W9-AUI-613

Hanging on the Wire

HANGING ON THE WIRE

GILLIAN LINSCOTT

St. Martin's Press
New York

Library of Congress Cataloging-in-Publication Data

Linscott, Gillian.
Hanging on the wire / Gillian Linscott.
p.   cm.
ISBN 0-312-08806-X
1. World War, 1914–1918—Fiction.   I. Title.
PR6062.I54H36   1993
823'.914—dc20   92-33295   CIP

First Published in Great Britain by Little, Brown and
Company.

First U.S. Edition: January 1993
10 9 8 7 6 5 4 3 2 1

The author would like to thank the staff of the Imperial War Museum, London, for their generous help with matters of fact. They bear no responsibility for the matter of fiction.

Hanging on the Wire

ONE

ONCE THE WORST OF THE riot was over I managed to read the letter from Jenny Chesney. I was sitting on the roof of a Birmingham meeting hall at the time, along with a pugnacious pacifist called Arthur Ricks, and a crowd of munitions workers were shouting insults at us from below. The letter had arrived by the early post that morning in June 1917, just before I'd set out from my home in Hampstead to speak at a Stop the War rally organised by the Midlands branch of the Women's International League. I'd stuffed it into my pocket, intending to read it later.

Since then, I'd had no time to spare for it. Some people in Birmingham were doing very well out of the war. Our rally had been disrupted by toughs sent along by the owners of local munitions factories, most of them well primed in the pubs, in spite of the law that said you weren't allowed to stand people rounds of drinks in case it sapped the war effort. Rotten vegetables flew, but we were used to that and had kept going. It was only when they were followed by lumps of wood and metal and a cohort of munitions workers stormed the platform that we decided to call a halt. Arthur, who is built like an omnibus, managed to keep the crowd at bay with a chair long enough for our main speaker, Ramsay Macdonald, to escape through a ground-floor window. When that route was cut off, Arthur and I took refuge on the flat roof, via the balcony and fire escape.

Now, as the long summer evening settled over the smoky roofs of Birmingham, Arthur had his arm hooked

1

round a flagpole and was leaning out, trying to reason with the crowd below at the top of his voice.

'Twenty thousand dead – on the first day of the Somme. How many more – do you want?'

The reply floated up from below.

'Hang the Hun lovers.'

Arthur turned and grinned at me.

'I think they're getting tired. You quite comfortable, Nell?'

'Quite comfortable, thank you Arthur. We can wait. It won't be dark for two hours yet.' I settled my back against a chimney stack and took Jenny's letter out of my pocket. She wasn't a close friend, but we'd met from time to time at meetings and rallies during the campaign for the Vote. I remembered her as a live-wire of a woman in her mid-twenties with a mass of honey-coloured hair, good-looking enough to disconcert men who thought all suffragettes must be old hags. Since then the outbreak of war had split the suffrage movement down the middle and set half of us at odds with the other half. Now as I and others travelled up and down the country appealing for an end to the war, our paths crossed with our former leaders', Emmeline and Christabel Pankhurst, addressing rallies to send more trainloads of machine-gun fodder to the trenches in France and Flanders. I'd lost touch with Jenny and didn't know which side she was on, but at least the opening of her letter made that clear.

'Dear Nell,

I read about your activities. Thank goodness some of us are trying to stop this madness. I've been seeing some of the effects of it. I'm working as an assistant at a small auxiliary hospital for shell-shocked cases in Wales. It's an experimental unit, run by a man called Dr Julius Stroud. He's financing it himself, so the War Office have to put up with us for the present, but they'd like to close us because they think we're not getting men back to the fighting quickly enough. That's why I'm so worried about what's been

2

happening here over the past few weeks and very much need help. I'm writing to you because I remembered that Mrs Pankhurst dropped some complimentary hints about a peculiar business in Biarritz you were involved in some time ago . . .'

I laughed. It had indeed been some time ago and Emmeline Pankhurst had been less complimentary since. The last time we'd met, in the booking hall at Euston station, she'd hissed 'Traitor' and swept past with her nose in the air. I read on.

'. . . and I know you can be quite tactful when you try, in spite of what people say. For the past two months or so we've been under attack from an appalling war-mongering woman called Monica Minter, who's staying near here. She's a leading light in something called the Duty and Discipline Movement and seems to have got it into her head that we are all German agents. She used to be in the suffrage movement and must have heard of you, so perhaps if you came here you could see her and reason with her.'

Jenny seemed to have spacious ideas about disposing of my time. I glanced at the address on her letter: Nantgarrew, near Llanvihangel Crucorney, near Abergavenny, Monmouthshire. It would take me several days to pronounce the place, let alone go to it. There was one more page.

'But that's not the worst of it. Yesterday somebody shot at us. We don't know who it was. Dr Stroud and two of the patients were in a conservatory at the back of the house and they might have been killed. Dr Stroud is firmly against involving the police in any way because it would disturb our patients and make complications with the War Office. So if you could find two or three days to come here and see if you can find out anything, I'd be eternally grateful. Only, if you come, it might be best if we let it be known that you're a friend of mine who's interested in Dr Stroud's work. Please come if you can.

Yours, in hope,
Jenny Chesney.'

Arthur was still carrying on his discussion with the voices forty feet below. I waited for a lull.

'Arthur, have you heard of a Dr Julius Stroud?'

He knew an amazing variety of people.

'Yes. Neurologist. Done some very interesting work. He went out to Vienna and studied with Dr Freud for some time. You know, the dreams man.'

My knowledge of the work of Dr Freud was hazy. I find that people who spend too much time worrying about their own minds seldom have minds worth worrying about. Still, at least it proved that Jenny's letter wasn't entirely fantasy.

'What about the Duty and Discipline Movement?'

'Peculiar. Put out pamphlets telling people to send their gardeners to fight in the trenches, that sort of thing.'

I re-read Jenny's letter. It was warm on the roof and in spite of the voices below, quite peaceful. If I rearranged my work I might be able to spend a couple of days in Wales before final preparations for the big Manchester rally.

Arthur strolled over to me.

'There aren't many of them left, Nell, and there's another fire escape down to a side street. Shall we try it?'

We tried it. According to the newspapers, women's skirts had risen to an astonishing six inches above the ground because of the demands of war work. As we scrambled down, it struck me that it came in useful for anti-war work as well. I wondered whether I dared adopt trousers like the women wore in the munitions factories, but supposed that would be considered tactless. When we got down to the side street – with the opposition round at the front still baying to the roof for our blood – we ran for the railway station. The newspaper placards there read: 'Allies Control Messines Ridge'. People said it would be all over by Christmas. Which was what they'd said three years ago. Arthur and I parted, he to go back to Leeds, I to London.

After seeing him off, I had an hour to wait for my train. There were a group of young soldiers on the platform, on their way back to France after leave. They sat on their kit-bags in the warm dusk. One of them had a mouth organ and they sang as he played, not the songs of the patriotic rallies but the doleful, stoic soldiers' songs from the trenches. There was one in particular that stuck in my mind:

'When you're hanging on the wire, Never Mind.
When you're hanging on the wire, Never Mind.
Though the light's as bright as day,
When you die they stop your pay.
When you're hanging on the wire, Never Mind.'

TWO

WAR-WOUNDED MEN WERE EVERYWHERE in the long summer day's journey to Wales. At Paddington, women medical orderlies and volunteers with tea wagons were waiting for the arrival of a hospital train. At Newport, the first city the train came to in Wales, there was a big military hospital. I had to change there, and while I was waiting for the local train to Abergavenny I watched convalescent patients, in their blue hospital uniforms, out strolling in the sunshine in a public park. Of the men who came home wounded, three-quarters were declared cured and returned for duty to the hell-holes that had hurt them in the first place. I looked at the nurses, as they watched their walking patients, and was angry that their care and gentleness should be used in such a cause. If I could help Jenny in keeping even a few men out of the clutches of the War Office, then my time would not be wasted.

When I got out at Abergavenny I found there were no buses from there to Llanvihangel Crucorney. Luckily before I left London I'd taken the precaution of changing into walking skirt and shoes and packing my things into a haversack. I'd had a lot to do that morning before I could leave, so it was early evening before I asked for directions and started my walk along the dusty road. The heat of the day was over. High green hills rose on either side of me as I walked, with patches of woodland and scattered farmhouses set well back from the road. There was a smell of hay in the air, and the bleats of half-grown lambs.

About three miles out from Abergavenny a flat farm cart caught up with me. It was drawn by a brown cob and driven by a middle-aged farmer with a placid face, wearing tweed jacket, breeches and gaiters.

'Good evening, ma'am. Would you be the lady who was asking for Nantgarrew?'

I said I was, not surprised that the arrival of a stranger should be public knowledge in such a quiet place.

'They said at the station you'd been asking. If you don't mind the cart, I could give you a ride as far as Cymyoy.'

His voice was as Welsh as Cadwallader. I thanked him and got up beside him.

'Are you a nurse, ma'am?'

'No. I'm visiting a friend who works as Nantgarrew. Her name's Jenny Chesney.'

He beamed.

'I know about Miss Jenny, she's the one who helps the doctors. Gwenda's very fond of Miss Jenny.'

'Gwenda?'

'My daughter. She used to work in the kitchen there. Doesn't any more.'

His smile faded.

We came round the side of a hill into a deeper valley with steep hills on either side and a stream running down beside the road. The cob paced on, with no guidance from the slack reins, as the farmer talked.

'I hear they had a bit of a scare up there last Sunday. Somebody nearly shot.'

'What happened?'

I thought Jenny wouldn't be pleased to know it was the talk of the valley.

'We heard about it from the lad who does their garden. Apparently it was one of them doing a bit of target practice, only it went off target like.'

'I thought it was a hospital. Do they usually do target practice?'

'Well, it's not an ordinary kind of hospital, is it? It's for people hurt in their nerves. I suppose they have to keep their hands in for when they get sent back to the fighting. Though, as I said to Gwenda, if that's what their aim's like, I don't see them doing much harm to the Germans.'

7

A group of grey buildings came in sight about half a mile away up the road.

'That's my place. I'll have to put you down there because I've got the cows to milk before dark, but Nantgarrew's only two miles on from there.'

The sun was balancing on the top of the hills, filling the valley with golden light. Up the road there was a dust cloud coming towards us. When it got nearer, we could see it was a khaki-coloured motor wagon.

'Is that from Nantgarrew?'

'Yes. It will be taking some of the men back. Eight of them going back today, the lad said.'

'Back where?'

'Back to the big hospital in Newport, then to the war.'

The wagon came nearer, towards the farm turning. I could see a small figure standing there by the road. As the wagon passed it waved and waved, so vigorously that it almost fell over. I looked at the farmer's face, about to ask who it was, and stopped myself. The wagon came on, past us. The men inside it, in their khaki uniforms, were sitting on the floor or standing and clinging on to the sides. They waved and shouted as they passed, called goodbye to the farmer, some even raised their hats to me, then they were gone in the dust cloud down the valley.

When we got to the farmer's drive, the girl who'd waved at the wagon was still standing there. Tears were pouring down her cheeks.

'Go in Gwenda. No good waiting here.'

The farmer's voice was gentle. He added something in Welsh. She glanced at us, turned, then ran away up the drive, made clumsy by misery. Her father watched her for a while, sighed, then held the horse steady while I got down.

'You just keep straight . . .'

Another vehicle came down the valley, much faster, horn tooting at us. It was a red motor car that must have been doing at least twenty miles an hour. The driver made no attempt to slow down as it passed us and the cloud of dust it stirred up made the cob snort. I had just a glimpse

8

of the person at the wheel, a woman in a long brown motoring coat, goggles and a tricorn hat, tied firmly down with a long red scarf to match the car. She was sitting very straight and upright, as if riding a hunter.

I said: 'Would that by any chance be Monica Minter?'

He gave me a sideways look.

'Yes. Do you know her?'

'No. My friend mentioned her.'

'She stays with her aunt at the next house up past us. She's a very strong-minded lady.'

His tone was cautious.

'I gather she doesn't like the people at Nantgarrew.'

'Her husband's a captain in the Navy, up in the Atlantic looking for submarines. She lost her brother at the Somme.'

He seemed determined not to commit himself. He handed me down my haversack.

'Just keep straight along this road for two miles or so. Don't take the first turning on the right, that's the road up to the old quarry. Half a mile past that, you'll see a waterfall coming straight down and a big white house near the bottom of it in some trees, well back from the road. That's Nantgarrew.'

For the first half-hour or so I followed his directions, then I got lost. There must have been a turning he hadn't allowed for in his directions, or perhaps I'd mistaken the subtle difference between grassy track that didn't count and a grassy road that did. In any case, the result was that I wasted the next half hour on the road I shouldn't have taken and found myself at the foot of the quarry, then another hour trying to take what looked like a short cut back to the road. By the time I'd scrambled over half a dozen dry stone walls, scattered several flocks of yelling sheep and floundered up to my ankles in a patch that even in midsummer contrived to be boggy I was ready to curse Jenny, Nantgarrew and all its works. It was dusk when I got back to the road, almost dark when I saw a gash of gold against the hillside that turned out to be a narrow waterfall reflecting the last glint of the sun and a square white house below it. It was set close against the steep hillside, its back huddled into a thicket of rhododendrons and birches. A winding drive led towards it from the road with pasture fields on either side, through a narrow opening in a high grassy bank. A sign on the gate said 'Nantgarrew' but there was nothing to show it was anything other than a private house.

That morning I'd telegraphed to Jenny to expect me by dinner time. Even if the telegraph had reached her in such a remote place, she'd surely have given me up for the day. I closed the gate behind me and began to walk up the drive, tired and hungry, hoping there'd be some dinner left. As I came close to the bank it looked as if it might be an ancient earthwork, built up to make a modern boundary. There was a ditch below it, then a few yards of rough grass and a barbed wire fence, dividing the grounds of the house from the fields. It was a very elaborate fence, coils of barbed wire nailed to thick wooden stakes, far more than needed to keep sheep out. It looked alien and threatening in the half-light. The drive ran through an opening in the wire, then through a gap in the bank, over a cattle grid. For a small auxiliary hospital, Nantgarrew seemed alarmingly well defended. I paused at the cattle grid to adjust my pack, looking back down to the darkening valley.

'Halt, who goes there?'

I jumped round. The voice had come from behind the bank, a cultivated voice, but nervy. I took a step forward.

'Identify yourself, friend or foe?'

I could see somebody now, a head and shoulders in silhouette. Jenny might have warned me about military guards.

'My name's Nell Bray. I'm expected. Jenny Chesney invited me.'

A man appeared in the gap in the bank. He was tall and thin and although, as far as I could see in the dusk, he wasn't wearing uniform he held himself very straight. Then another voice behind him, less nervous and obviously Yorkshire.

'What's up, sir? Who have you got there?'

'It's a woman.'

The first man's voice made that sound like a crime in itself.

'The mad woman?'

'No, another one. She says Miss Chesney invited her.'

The second man came scrambling down the bank towards me.

'Evening ma'am, sorry you've been troubled. Don't worry about the lady, sir. I'll escort her up to the house.'

He was short and square and his voice was cheerful. He hoisted the pack from my shoulders on to his own and gave me an arm to help me over the cattle grid, not that I needed it. The taller man fell back to let us through.

The house had been hidden by the bank but it came into sight again as we walked up the drive, lights shining in some of its windows.

'My name's Jack Kelso. Most people call me Jacko. I hope Captain Hunter didn't scare you, Miss.'

'Do you always keep a guard on the house?'

'Well, you couldn't call it a guard exactly. It's mainly the Captain and me, and a few of the others when he can persuade them to do it. But we've had a bit of trouble here lately and Captain Hunter feels responsible.'

'Responsible?'

'He isn't, not in any sensible way. But he had a bad time out there and it left him feeling he's letting people down all the time. Dr Stroud says it's something to do with his mother.'

'I'd have thought it was more likely to do with the war.'

'To be honest with you, Miss, so would I. But it's interesting what the doctor digs up sometimes.'

'Why is there barbed wire all round the place?'

He glanced at me.

'It's not all round, you'll see tomorrow. Only this bit by the drive and up round the corner into the field. The Captain wants it all round, but it's not easy getting hold of the wire.'

'But if it's not all round, couldn't anybody get in where

11

there's no wire?'

'Yes Miss, and they do.'

He sounded quite unconcerned about it.

'Then why go to all the trouble to have a piece of fence and a guard?'

'It's something for me and Captain Hunter to do. It makes him feel calmer in his mind.'

I thought I was beginning to get my bearings. The cheerful Jack Kelso was obviously an orderly or male nurse and Captain Hunter was one of the patients. I asked him if he'd been at Nantgarrew long.

'Four months. They sent me up here in March.'

'Were you working at another hospital before that?'

'Oh no, Miss, I'm not one of the staff. I'm one of the patients. Sergeant Kelso, at your service.'

He grinned, led the way up the steps to the front door and rang the bell. It was an imposing porch with pillars on either side and two shadowy animals, lions probably, guarding the steps.

'The door isn't locked, but we'd better let them know you're here.'

As we waited for an answer to the bell, he asked me if I'd seen anybody else on my walk.

'Not since I left Cymyoy.'

'I just wondered if you'd come across Beethoven. He's gone off on one of his hikes again. Nobody's seen him since breakfast.'

The door opened and, to my relief, there was Jenny standing in the lamplight.

THREE

'NELL, WHAT TOOK YOU SO LONG?'

Jenny came rushing down the steps and took me by the hand. She was wearing a grey dress of severe design, her hair tucked up in a tight pleat at the back. Even by lamplight I could see that she was tired and strained. A large man was standing behind her in the doorway.

'Nell, may I introduce Dr Julius Stroud. Dr Stroud, this is my friend Nell Bray.'

He smiled and took my hand.

'You're very welcome, Miss Bray.'

His voice was deep and pleasant with the slightest of burrs in it, Lincolnshire possibly, or Norfolk. Somewhere of level fields and wide skies. I don't know why I'd expected a neurologist to be small and slight. Julius Stroud was nothing of the kind. He must have been around six feet tall with broad shoulders and a thatch of brown hair just flecked with grey, not very well cut. He was bearded, but it was a square, countryman's beard. If I'd met him without knowing his profession I'd probably have taken him for a farmer. The only visible touch of the academic was a pair of wire-framed spectacles.

Jack Kelso had put down my pack inside the door and disappeared. The hall was lit by two lamps on brackets and there was a smell of paraffin. Dr Stroud paused by a door on the right of the hall.

'I'm sure you and Jenny will want to talk, Miss Bray. If you'll excuse me, I have notes to write up. I'll be happy to talk to you about our work here tomorrow, when you've had a chance to rest.'

13

As the door closed behind him, Jenny could hardly contain her relief at seeing me.

'I'd almost given you up, Nell. Thank goodness you're here.'

'Why, has something else happened?'

'No, but it's been a bad day. They've just taken eight patients away from us and . . . Oh Nell, I'm so confused.'

'I think I saw your patients going down the valley. There was a girl from a farm waving to them.'

Jenny bit her lip.

'Oh dear, that must have been poor Gwenda. I'll tell you about that later. But you must be starving. Your room's next to mine. I'll show you up and see about something to eat for you.'

The room Jenny had prepared for me was comfortable but simply furnished, a narrow bed with a patchwork cover, a washstand with basin and ewer, a small table supporting a paraffin lamp and a box of lucifers.

'Let me light it for you. We haven't got gas here, let alone electricity.'

When she'd gone I went over to the window. It looked out from the back of the house to the waterfall and the steep slope of the hill. The moon was rising, almost a full one. The slopes above and to the side of the house were dotted with rocks and sheep. Until one of them moved, it was hard to tell which was which. A dark shrubbery of rhododendrons came almost to the back of the house and just below me was the glass roof of a conservatory. I assumed that was where the shooting had happened. I washed in cold, moss-smelling water from the ewer and had just changed my blouse when Jenny came back.

'I've put your supper in my room. There's a bigger table.'

She'd set out a steaming jug of cocoa and two cups, cheese, cold mutton and pickles, slices of dark fruit loaf spread with rich butter. After the austerities of voluntary rationing in London, cafés where even the rock cake with your tea had to confine itself to a standard two ounces, it was a welcome sight. I asked Jenny to tell me about the shooting, but she said she'd wait until I'd eaten. She sat there on the bed, full of tension, looking at me over the rim of her cocoa cup as I ate.

'Tell me about Gwenda then. Her father said she worked in the kitchen here.'

Jenny nodded. 'Yes, until she fell in love with one of our patients and got pregnant by him. He was one of the people in the wagon you saw.'

'And now he's being sent back to the war.'

'Yes. Dr Stroud tried to convince the medical board he wasn't ready, which he isn't. But an awful man called Brigadier Moss was chairman of the board. He'd got to hear about it somehow, and he said if the man was well enough to make girls pregnant he was well enough to go and fight.'

She sipped her cocoa gloomily.

'It doesn't improve our prospects either. He made it very clear to Dr Stroud that if anything like that happened again, we'd be closed.'

'Where does this Brigadier Moss come from?'

'Down in Newport, where the main hospital is. We're officially an auxiliary hospital attached to it, but we're so far away that he doesn't often come here, thank goodness. But he doesn't like Dr Stroud and he'd love an excuse to close us.'

'How many patients are here?'

'We can take twenty, but we're down to twelve now those eight you saw have gone. We've only got two doctors here, Dr Stroud and Dr Caspian, and Freudian analysis takes a lot of time. That's one of the things Brigadier Moss refuses to understand. And we're a constant irritation to him because Dr Stroud refuses to run Nantgarrew on military lines.'

'No uniforms?'

'No, and as few distinctions as possible between ranks. Officially Dr Stroud and Dr Caspian are majors in the medical corps for the duration of the war. Brigadier Moss made a terrible row when he found they were forbidding patients to say "Sir" to them.'

15

'Who won?'

'Oh, Dr Stroud mainly. When Brigadier Moss visits, everybody throws a few "Sirs" around to make him happy, then we go back to normal.'

'Jack Kelso called Captain Hunter "Sir".'

'Oh, you've met Hal Hunter?'

'I could hardly avoid it. I gather he's pining for more barbed wire fences.'

'Yes. Dr Stroud says it's a classic symptom of repression and what he's really doing is mounting guard on his own subconscious.'

I let that pass for the while.

'I took Jack Kelso for one of the staff at first, but it's obvious he's very confused, poor man.'

She stared.

'Sergeant Jacko? But he's not confused at all. He's making a very good recovery.'

'I'm afraid he's had a relapse. He started talking about Beethoven and wanted to know if I'd seen him.'

She laughed with relief.

'Oh, that's all right. Beethoven's the men's name for one of our patients. He plays the piano beautifully.'

'And goes off on long walks?'

'Yes, all night sometimes. That's one of his neurotic symptoms, like Hal Hunter and his barbed wire. And this persecution from Monica Minter isn't helping.'

I finished the last slice of currant bread.

'Right, now about this shooting.'

Jenny put her cup down and took a deep breath.

'It was three days ago, just before tea on Sunday afternoon, about four-thirty. Dr Stroud was waiting in his study because a man named Lieutenant Stanley Gorton was due for a session of analysis. He was late, and I thought I'd seen him going into the conservatory with Colonel Keyson. So we went to look for him.'

'*Colonel* Keyson?'

She looked uneasy.

'Yes, officially he outranks everybody here, but he's a patient like everybody else.'

She had her hands clasped together and the fingers were straining against each other.

'Go on.'

'There are two doors into the conservatory, one from the house, the other from outside. Naturally, we went through the house. I was in the corridor just behind Dr Stroud when he opened the conservatory door. That was when it happened.'

'What happened exactly?'

'He'd just started saying something to Stanley Gorton when there was a crack and a sound of glass breaking. He rushed into the conservatory and I went after him. There was Stanley Gorton crouched down behind the wooden staging and Ralph Keyson standing there looking out at the shrubbery. He said: "Somebody's taken a shot at him." Then he dashed out of the door and I went after him. Dr Stroud had to stay and look after Stanley Gorton. He was in a state of hysteria.'

'Why did you and Colonel Keyson dash out?'

'He was sure the shot was fired from the shrubbery. It must have been. We thought we could catch whoever fired it.'

'Wasn't that risky? He or she might have still been there.'

'I didn't think of that. I was just so angry.'

'But you didn't find anybody?'

'No. Whoever it was must have escaped through the shrubbery and into the fields.'

'Did you think to look for the bullet?'

'Yes. When we went back inside Ralph Keyson found it in the wall of the conservatory. It wasn't far from where poor Stanley Gorton had been standing.'

'How far?'

'He thought it had missed him by inches. He said he heard the whoosh of it going past his ear. It was probably nowhere near that close, perhaps five or six feet or so.'

'What kind of bullet?'

'The kind fired from a standard officer's revolver.'

'Do they keep their guns here?'

'Of course not. We're a hospital.'

'Gwenda's father seemed to think somebody had been doing target practice.'

'That's the story we put about down the valley. We knew we hadn't much hope of keeping it quiet altogether. All we can do is hope it doesn't get down as far as Newport.'

'Did you ask the staff and patients at the time if they knew anything?'

'We asked the two nurses, and Dr Caspian and the domestic staff, but they hadn't seen anything. We didn't cross-question the patients, but I think they all knew about it. They'd have said something if they'd seen anyone in the shrubbery.'

'You're sure it couldn't be some twisted kind of joke?'

'Who'd play a joke like that?'

'What about Mrs Monica Minter?'

'Oh, if only we could prove that, Nell. It would be such a relief.'

'Why?'

'Because it would be somebody from outside.'

'And you're afraid it might have been somebody from inside?'

'Nell, I don't know what to think. That's why I wrote to you. I've been thinking about it so much that my mind's knotted up with it.'

'What does Dr Stroud think?'

'He says it's not part of Mrs Minter's pattern. Up to now they've been silly, hurtful things she's done, but not dangerous. Not physically dangerous, at any rate.'

'What sort of things?'

'The first thing, about six weeks ago, she draped a big banner over the gate at the bottom of the drive: "The Kaiser's Rest Home for Nervous Soldiers". Luckily the garden boy found it before any of the patients saw it but . . .'

'Would it have bothered them?'

'It was so desperately unfair. Then she started making wild allegations that we were part of a plot to undermine national morale. Apparently because Dr Freud's an Austrian and Austria's on the same side as the Germans anybody who's interested in Freud's theories must be an enemy agent. The result was that we had a policeman up all the way from Cardiff asking silly questions. Then there were the feathers.'

'White feathers?'

'Yes. She drove straight up the drive one night and tipped a laundry basket full of them all over the front steps. We were wading in them. She must have raided every poultry yard from here to the sea.'

'Did any of the men see that?'

'Jack Kelso and Beethoven.'

'Were they upset?'

'Well, not on the face of it. In fact, they seemed to think it was a great joke. But you know what Dr Freud says about jokes.'

'No.'

'That pleasure in a joke arises from the temporary suspension of the effort involved in maintaining repression.'

'Ye gods, I hope I never have to sit next to him at dinner.'

Jenny gave me a hurt, disappointed look, the kind a believer gives sceptics at a seance. I registered that, for my stay at Nantgarrew, jokes about Dr Freud were tactless.

'Anyway, I can see what Dr Stroud means. There's a considerable distance between that sort of silliness and actually shooting at somebody. There's one obvious question for a start.'

'What's that?'

'Whether whoever fired the shot really intended to hit somebody, and if so, who? Have you any ideas on that?'

'Well . . .'

She was twisting a fold of the bedcover in her fingers, looking down at it.

'Come on, you must have some idea?'

'It's difficult.'

I sighed. Whatever Nantgarrew might be doing for its patients, it seemed to be having a bad effect on Jenny.

'We'll take them one at a time, then. You say the bullet

19

might have passed within five feet of Lieutenant Stanley Gorton. Was anybody else closer?'

She shook her head.

'No. Dr Stroud in the doorway would have been the next nearest, but he was at least double the distance away.'

'So if this person was trying to shoot somebody in particular, the inference is that it was Lieutenant Gorton, unless he or she was a very bad shot.'

'Yes, but I don't believe anybody here would want to shoot Stanley Gorton.'

'Why? Is he so lovable?'

'No, not in the least. The general effect is pathetic. He's going bald and he walks with a limp because he had a piece of shrapnel in his leg and the only things he's interested in are watching birds and eating. He's a mass of repressions, of course.'

'So it must follow that the target, if there was one, was Dr Stroud or Colonel Keyson. Tell me about this Keyson.'

Jenny didn't look at me as she spoke.

'He's young for a Colonel, only thirty-seven. He was in the army before the war started, a career soldier. He's only been with us for a month.'

The way she talked about him was quite different from the way she'd talked about Stanley Gorton. I suspected that she was trying hard to seem unemotional, and warned myself to tread carefully for once.

'What's wrong with him?'

'He was sent home from France in the first place for an operation for a perforated ulcer. Then, when he was supposed to be recovering, he started having really bad screaming nightmares, so they sent him to us. Dr Stroud thinks the anaesthetic for the operation might have released memories he was trying to hide from himself.'

'Is he recovering?'

'Oh, it's early days yet. Of course, it's not easy for him here, because of his rank.'

'I suppose he finds it difficult mingling on social terms with mere NCOs.'

Jenny ignored the sarcasm.

20

'It's worse than that, Nell. He's a staff officer.'

She dropped her voice when she said it, as well she might. If there was one group of people the soldier in the trenches hated worse than the Germans it was his own staff officers, tucked away safely in headquarters behind the lines, sending wave after wave of men to be killed.

'Well, if somebody's taken a shot at him, I shouldn't be in the least surprised.

'Nell, don't be cruel. Staff officers have feelings too. That's why he's here.'

'Do the others have much to do with him?'

'Not much, except Beethoven suddenly launched into him at breakfast last week. He accused Keyson of killing some of his friends. After that, Beethoven just disappeared for two days. Luckily he brought himself back before we had to inform Brigadier Moss that he was missing.'

'Where was this Beethoven when the shot was fired?'

'Out walking, I suppose. He usually is.'

I tried to get the situation in the conservatory clear in my mind.

'But the fact seems to be that even if Beethoven or anybody else might have wanted to shoot Colonel Keyson, he was actually the furthest away.'

'Yes, twenty feet at least. I've paced it out.'

'I'm glad to see your brain hasn't given up entirely. So if somebody was aiming for Colonel Keyson, it was an absurdly bad shot. What about Dr Stroud? I assume nobody wants to kill him.'

'Well, not consciously.'

I stared at her.

'You mean somebody might want to kill Dr Stroud unconsciously?'

Again, she took my sarcasm at face value.

'What I mean is that a patient might, in theory, want to kill Dr Stroud without actually wanting to kill him.'

I stood up.

'Jenny Chesney, unless you start making better sense than this, I'm going straight back home, even if I have to walk all the way to Abergavenny by moonlight.'

She saw that I meant it, and got off the bed ready to try and stop me.

'Nell, I'm sorry, I'm trying, I really am.'

'Well, sit down, take a deep breath and try again.'

She took several.

'The point is that in Freudian psychoanalysis the patient will almost invariably make a transference. That is to say, at some stage he'll come to regard the analyst as a parent, usually the father.'

'But people don't normally want to kill their fathers.'

'Oh yes they do, Nell. That's what the Oedipus Complex is all about.'

'Oedipus Complex?'

'Surely you know about it, Nell. It's the very keystone of Dr Freud's work.'

'Jenny, I've been quite busy lately. You know, the Vote, the war and so on.'

She was as impervious as a religious convert.

'You must do some reading, Nell, or you won't understand our work here.'

She went to her bookcase and came back with two forbidding volumes.

'Freud's *Totem and Taboo*. Do you want it in English or German?'

I opted for German. It's a language that flatters inanities.

'So what you're telling me is that according to the theories Dr Stroud works by, a patient might regard him as a father and want to kill him.'

'Yes.'

'Any patient?'

'In theory, yes.'

'And there were twenty patients here before the eight left today.'

'Yes, but only six of them in full Freudian psychoanalysis.'

I felt my head swimming. It had been a long day. I took a steadying gulp of cold cocoa.

'Explain.'

'As I told you, Nell, it takes a lot of time. With just two doctors we can't give twenty patients full analysis. Dr Caspian treats most of them on a basis of modified Freudian methods, with Dr Stroud in overall charge of their treatment. Dr Stroud himself takes six of the most serious cases for daily analysis sessions. Of all the war hospitals, we're the only one where full Freudian psychoanalysis is being used.'

At least it was probably better than in the trenches.

'So, this transference business, is it most likely to happen to one of the six?'

'Yes.'

'Are all six of them still here?'

'Yes. You've met Jack Kelso and Hal Hunter. I've told you about Ralph Keyson, Stanley Gorton and Beethoven. That only leaves Robin Duncan. They call him Red Robin on account of his politics.'

'Is he an officer?'

'Good heavens, no. He's a corporal. He regards all officers as enemies of the working class. Robin is very young, very Scottish and very argumentative.'

'Had he shown any signs of carrying on his argument with guns?'

'No, but neither have the others.'

'Coming back to Mrs Minter, have we any reason to think that she might want to shoot anybody in particular?'

'Well, Dr Stroud I suppose. As she sees it, he's the head traitor.'

'But she couldn't have known that Dr Stroud was going to walk into the conservatory while she was conveniently waiting with a gun in the shrubbery.'

'Unless she'd been lurking there all afternoon. Anything's possible with that woman.'

I sat up for some time after leaving Jenny, making notes on what she'd told me, wondering about what she hadn't told me. When a clear mind like Jenny's takes to dithering, there's usually a man involved somewhere. I remembered how nervous she'd seemed when talking about Colonel Keyson and filed that in my mind, although not in my notes, as a possible complication. Possibly, even, the reason why she'd summoned me so urgently.

Before I went to bed I went over to the window for another look down at the moonlit conservatory and the rhododendron shrubbery, trying to imagine the state of mind of somebody waiting there with a gun. Madness? Some people would say that all the patients were mad, that they wouldn't be at Nantgarrew otherwise. I didn't believe that. They weren't mad men, but they'd all been through experiences that would twist the sanest brain. Not mad, but cheated of some part of their minds and left out there in a no-man's land between the barbed wire barricades of the sane and the insane. As I fell asleep, I was thinking of something Jack Kelso had said: 'It's not easy getting hold of the wire.'

FOUR

I WOKE BEFORE SIX TO sunlight and the sound of the waterfall. The hill behind the house was still in shadow but the air was already warm. It was too fine to go back to sleep so I dressed and went downstairs as quietly as I could. The key had been left on the inside of the front door, showing that Dr Stroud didn't think it necessary to lock up his patients. I walked round to the front of the house. Across the valley and up and down it was nothing but sheep pasture climbing to deeper patches of bracken then, on the very tops of the hills, outcrops of red rock. No other house was visible. Cymyoy, where Gwenda and her father lived, was down towards Abergavenny, round a bend in the road.

The stretch of road immediately below the house was hidden by the earth bank where Captain Hunter had been keeping watch. Part of his barbed wire fence was visible where it turned a corner and ran steeply uphill for twenty yards or so. Then it stopped abruptly and gave place to an ordinary farm fence of wooden posts and rails, slanting and silver-grey with age, hardly enough to keep out a determined sheep. Nearer at hand some effort had gone into keeping up the grounds. I was standing on a terrace in front of French windows. Below me a roughly-cut lawn sloped to a paved area with a flagpole at one end of it and a bench and sundial in the middle. Beyond that were the rudiments of an herbaceous border, then the earth bank.

A path led from the terrace to the back of the house and the conservatory. The outside door of the conservatory was locked so I walked along the narrow path between the building and the rhododendrons. One of the panes had been recently replaced just to the left of centre, about four feet from the ground. The putty around it was still soft, with a linseed oil smell, and a few tiny splinters of glass glittered on the path where I was standing. Under the thick leaves of the rhododendrons there were no paths, only a jumble of rocks covered with dried moss. A few broken twigs and withered leaves suggested that somebody had pushed through them recently, but that might have been Colonel Keyson and Jenny, after the shot was fired.

The surprise was that it couldn't have been easy to shoot from the shrubbery. Rhododendrons are dense things and when I clambered over the rocks and sat down amongst them I found it difficult at first to pick out the new conservatory window. When I'd found it, the angle puzzled me. To put a bullet through the conservatory at that level, if you hoped to hit somebody standing inside it, you'd need to be lying on your stomach, facing downhill. Also, unless your victim had been standing close up against the glass, it would have been difficult to see him. All this suggested to me that the shot was more likely to have been a warped joke or a general piece of intimidation than an attempt to kill somebody.

I fought my way out from among the leathery leaves to a flight of steps that led uphill beside the shrubbery. In the open, I glanced back towards the conservatory. What I saw there made me feel cold all down my spine. Somebody was watching me. He was standing there in khaki shirt and tie, all very correct, arms clasped behind him, staring out at me. From the way he was standing I thought he'd probably been there for some time and had watched me among the rhododendrons. He was quite a tall man with a large head the shape of an inverted acorn, very broad across the forehead with shadowy, deep-set eyes. His ears were rather prominent, his dark hair short and sleeked down. Altogether, not a comfortable looking man. The stare he was giving me was blank to the point of hostility.

I wasn't sure whether he was the other doctor or one of

the patients, but in either case it was his territory not mine. If the sight of me out walking early offended him, then I'd take myself off. I stared back just long enough to show I was aware of him, then went on up the steps and along a path that ran by the top of the shrubbery.

Here I was closer to the waterfall. It came clattering down with a noise like factory machinery and poured itself straight into a clump of hazels and stunted rowan trees with hardly a splash. I followed the path in that direction and found a deep pool with the waterfall crashing down into the far side of it. Even in the drought it was still loud enough to drive all other thoughts from my mind apart from how cool and inviting the pool looked. It was clear green, sur-rounded by flat rocks with ferns and ash seedlings growing up between them. At its deepest point it was quite broad enough to swim a stroke or two. I'd been too long in dusty cities to resist it. I scrambled out of my clothes, folded them on a rock and slid in. After the first shock of cold I swam and splashed for a while then stood up under the waterfall, letting it soak my hair.

If it hadn't been for the crashing of the waterfall I might have heard steps on the path. As it was, the first thing I was heard was a voice.

'Who's swimming? Is that you, Hal?'

It came from just the other side of the bushes.

'No, it's not Hal. Can you wait for a minute?'

But I was too late. A man was standing by the pool. A tall man, but stooping a little. Long legs and a brown face, creased into weary furrows. In his forties, but hair more grey than brown. But before all that I noticed that his eyes were full of fear. Not embarrassment, which would have been reasonable enough in the circumstances, but real fear as if he'd seen Medusa herself rising out of the pool. It seemed a long time before he said anything.

'Oh my God, I'm dreaming again. Nell Bray. Nell Bray drowning.'

Now it was my turn to feel scared. I stayed there under the waterfall as if it gave me some protection. I started to ask him how he knew my name. Then it hit me, far colder than the water.

'David. David Ellward.'

He turned away, shaking his head.

'David, don't worry, it really is me. And I'm not drowning, I'm just having a swim.'

It was no time for modesty. I scrambled out, pulled on clothes over wet skin, knotted up my soaking hair as best I could. By the time I'd finished he'd turned and was watching me. At first there was only puzzlement on his face, but then at last a smile that looked as if he'd kept it folded away for months.

'Is it really you, Nell?'

'I should have thought that was obvious in the last few minutes.'

'Was I staring? I'm sorry. Anyway, what in the world are you doing here?'

'Visiting Jenny Chesney. I assume you're . . .'

'One of Dr Stroud's patients? Just so.'

'You're the one they call Beethoven. You play the piano beautifully and go off on long walks and you . . . Oh, I should have guessed.'

We were sitting side by side on a rock. My grey flannel skirt hung clammily around my calves.

'I don't know why you should have guessed. I don't suppose you even knew I was in France, let alone invalided out.'

'I knew you'd volunteered.'

A mutual friend had told me this a year after the start of the war, adding that David's marriage had recently collapsed. I'd never known his wife.

'I suppose you said "The silly fool".'

'Yes. It seemed a self-destructive thing to do. You'd have been too old for conscription. You probably had to lie about your age to get in.'

'A lot of us did that. There was a man in my platoon who was over sixty.'

'Why did you do it?'

'Oh, you know, it seemed to simplify things at the time.'

He looked away from me, over the shrubbery to the

house. I noticed he was wearing heavy boots with nailed soles.

'Were you going out walking again?'

'Yes. I suppose Jenny told you that. It seems that's the way it takes me. I just need to keep walking.'

'Is that such a problem?'

He looked at me and smiled.

'It almost had me court-martialled and shot.'

'For walking?'

'At the wrong time in the wrong direction. You heard about the Battle of Arras, I suppose?'

'Thirty thousand men dead for a hundred yards of mud. You were there?'

He nodded.

'I'd come through the whole of the Somme business with nothing worse than a bit of shell casing in the shoulder. Every man in my platoon killed, and that happened twice over, but nothing seemed to touch me. Then they moved us up to Arras. I don't know what they told you people at home about that first morning, Nell. The tanks were supposed to be going in front, knocking out the machine guns for us. Then all of a sudden there were no tanks, nothing between us and the Germans. They'd held their fire till then, then they started. There was a lad walking next to me, no more than eighteen. He'd just begun to say, "Here Sir, this is a bit of all right". He managed the "all", didn't get as far as the "right".'

'And you?'

'Not a scratch. That night, back in our own trenches, I suddenly felt like going for a walk. I climbed out and just kept walking. The military police picked me up at dawn next morning, twenty miles behind our lines.'

'Where were you going?'

'Didn't know then, don't know now. But it counts as desertion in the face of the enemy. If I'd been a poor bloody private they'd probably have shot me. Since I wasn't they decided I was a suitable case for Dr Stroud.'

He told it in such a matter-of-fact, accepting way that I felt like screaming at him, making him share my anger.

29

Instead I asked him what he thought about Dr Stroud's methods, expecting scepticism or ridicule.

'He's an interesting man. I'm not sure that Freudianism will do the trick for me, but I'm sure there are people his methods could help. The central idea, as I understand it, is that the neuroses we suffer have their origins in the conflicts of early childhood.'

'Nothing to do with the war?'

'Perhaps it's the other way about and war comes from our unresolved conflicts.'

'In that case, shouldn't he be psychoanalysing Field-Marshal Haig?'

David smiled.

'I wonder what that man's dreams are like. It's one of the big things here, you know, dreams.'

'Is that why you thought you were dreaming when you saw me in the pool?'

'In the circumstances it seemed the most likely explanation.'

'But why did you think I was drowning?'

'Perhaps I unconsciously wanted to drown you.'

He seemed quite serious.

'Why should you want to do that?'

'Ah, I don't know, do I? Perhaps for not marrying me when I asked you to, all those years ago.'

'As far as I recall, you never asked me. Not properly. It was all in the subjunctive. "Supposing I thought you might consider . . .?" '

'Supposing I had?'

'There you go again. No, I don't suppose so.'

'I didn't think so.'

'There was so much else that needed doing.'

'With you there always was.'

By then the tension had broken and we were laughing at each other, not bitterly.

I said: 'I'm hungry. What time's breakfast?'

'Not for an hour or more.'

'Come and walk then. You can show me how a person could get into the rhododendron shrubbery from outside.'

30

'Oh, that's easy. We just take that little path through the bushes.'

We followed it and came to a dry stone wall, about chest height. The part of it where the path ended was low, with a flat stone over it making a kind of stile.

'Almost anybody could get over that, couldn't they?'

I had the old feeling that he was reading my thoughts.

'And before you ask, Nell, anybody could get here by walking across two fields from the road. So you see, it could have been Mrs Minter who fired that shot.'

'Do you think it was?'

'I've no idea. You're the detective.'

'Hardly that.'

'I wonder. You never used to be the sort of woman who paid casual visits to old friends and Jenny Chesney is a very worried lady.'

He said her name, I thought, a little wryly, as if he wasn't quite friends with her.

'Worried with reason?'

He shrugged.

We walked back between the bushes onto the wider path by the pool. The sun had come over the hill by then and dried the splashes on the rocks from my swim.

'Tell me, Nell, just after we met you were about to say something else you'd heard about me. I play the piano, I go for long walks and . . . And what?'

'And you got into an argument with Colonel Keyson.'

'Yes. I'm sorry about that. I shouldn't have done it.'

This new humility was worrying. The David I remembered had more than a touch of arrogance.

'I don't blame you for finding staff officers infuriating.'

'No. I mean I shouldn't have wasted time arguing. I should calmly and quietly have broken his bloody neck.'

He said it as evenly as if we were discussing a concert programme.

'You think I'm joking. I told you, I had a platoon killed round me twice over. The second time it was the direct result of an attack plan formulated by that bloody bastard. And if you don't believe me ask Hal Hunter or Jacko. They know all about it.'

In silence, we walked down the steps beside the shrubbery. When he spoke again we were back to the teasing tone.

'Any more detecting you want to do before breakfast?'

'I'm not sure there's a lot that I can do.'

As I said it the air was split by the sound of a whistle, blown long and shrill. Voices were shouting from the front of the house.

'Oh God, what's happened now?'

David set off round the house at a lope and I followed. One of the voices was shouting 'Stop her!'

FIVE

AS WE ROUNDED THE FRONT of the house a voice shouted down from the first floor.

'David, what's going on?'

It was Dr Stroud in striped pyjamas, leaning out of what was presumably his bedroom window. David stopped and looked up.

'The usual problem, I think.'

'Has she . . .? Oh yes, she has. Look at the flagpole.'

From the pole at the bottom of the lawn, a large white flag shifted slightly in the warm breeze. David said something under his breath. A man appeared from over the earthwork and marched up the lawn towards us. It was the man I'd first met the night before, Captain Hal Hunter. He was fully dressed in civilian clothes of trousers, shirt and tie, with a whistle on a cord looped through a buttonhole. He placed himself in the middle of the terrace and reported to Dr Stroud at the upstairs window.

'I observed her loitering suspiciously on the lawn. I immediately challenged her. She made her escape on a bicycle. Corporal Duncan is pursuing her, but the terrain gives an advantage to bicycles.'

Dr Stroud sighed. 'I'll come down.'

The three of us, Hunter, David and myself stood looking at each other.

I asked: 'Was it Monica Minter?' Hunter made a disgusted noise. I didn't know if it was at me, Mrs Minter or both. He turned on his heel and David and I followed him down the lawn, past the sundial and a big urn of geraniums, to the flagpole. The flag was a white bed sheet, not hoisted on ropes but nailed to the flagstaff about half-way up.

David said: 'Do you suppose she brought a step-ladder with her?' He sounded more amused than anything.

'She had her bicycle. I expect she leaned it against the flagpole and stood on the seat.'

It was the kind of thing I'd have done myself in a better cause. I asked Captain Hunter if anybody had seen her putting the flag up and this time he condescended to answer me.

'No. When I observed her she had her back to me and was bending over something on the lawn outside the windows of Dr Stroud's study.'

I went back there for a look, and the others followed, but we could see nothing out of the way.

Dr Stroud came to meet us. He'd changed out of his pyjamas into tweed trousers and a jersey.

'Has she done anything apart from the flag, Hal?'

'Not that I can ascertain.'

There were some leaflets scattered round the lawn. I picked one of them up. *Discipline and Training in the Prevention of Nervous Diseases*, published by the Duty and Discipline Movement. I handed one to Dr Stroud and he made a face. I left the three of them picking up the leaflets and strolled across the grass, accidentally kicking a watering can that had been left lying on its side near the flower border, under the windows. I decided that I would do what Jenny wanted and have a talk with Monica Minter. After hearing David's story I felt especially angry about her activities and although I didn't share Jenny's hope that I could persuade her to change her ways I at least intended to let her know what I thought about them.

A young man came running to join the others. He moved like an athlete and had a thatch of bright red hair. Even before I heard his Scots accent his youth identified him as Corporal Robin Duncan. He looked no older than twenty and I wondered what the war had done to him to send him to Nantgarrew.

'It was that Minter besom, not a doubt of it. I'd have got her, but she pedalled as if Old Nick was after her.'

He, like Hunter, made his report to Dr Stroud, but without any of the Captain's military formality.

Stroud said to him: 'What were you doing up so early, Robin? Trouble sleeping again?'

I saw Hunter wince when Stroud called Robin by his first name. The young man looked annoyed too, but more by Stroud's concern than anything else.

'I heard Mr Hunter blowing on his whistle, so I came down to see what was the trouble.'

There was a slight emphasis on the 'Mr'. He was clearly determined to annoy Hunter. You could see that he'd dressed in a hurry. He was wearing khaki sweater and trousers pulled on over pyjamas and his feet were bare.

Stroud said: 'You shouldn't have gone chasing off in bare feet. You've cut yourself.'

There was a long gash on his instep. He didn't even look down at it.

'It's better than having trench foot, isn't it – sir?'

The last word was said as an insult, but Stroud took no notice. Robin was even-handedly trying to annoy both his superiors.

Hunter said: 'I'm going to fetch a ladder and deal with that abomination.'

He waited as if for approval from Dr Stroud then, when nothing was said, turned and marched off.

Robin Duncan watched him go.

'Mr Hunter doesn't want it to be thought that we're surrendering. To the sheep, I suppose, since there's no other creature would be interested.' He glanced at me. 'Would that be a military offence do you suppose, Miss Bray? Cowardice in the face of sheep?'

I was aware of two things: an assurance remarkable in a young man and the fact that he already knew who I was. I said I supposed it would depend how hostile the sheep were.

'Perhaps Major Stroud could enlighten us.'

Again, Dr Stroud failed to rise to the bait. Robin gave us

both a look, head on one side, much like the bird he'd been named for, then walked quickly back to the house. There was no sign of a limp, though the cut on his instep must have hurt.

David, Dr Stroud and I followed more slowly.

I said: 'Corporal Duncan seems to have a selective attitude to military titles.'

'He only does it to annoy. He knows my attitude. Any kind of military hierarchy would be fatal to what we're trying to do here.'

'Captain Hunter doesn't seem to think so.'

'Hal insists on keeping up standards, as he calls it. It's clearly a necessary displacement of subsidiary neuroses for him at this stage.'

The words tripped more easily off his tongue than into my brain. I decided not to ask about them or he'd probably try to lend me a book as well. I'd tried a few pages of *Totem and Taboo* the night before and found them a powerful soporific.

'And I suppose annoying Captain Hunter is a necessary therapy for young Robin.'

'Oh, Robin doesn't approve of any of us. He thinks psychoanalysis is the latest diversion of a decadent bourgeoisie.'

'Then why is he here?'

Dr Stroud didn't answer.

David said: 'Robin's here for much the same reason as I am. It was either this or a firing squad for incitement to mutiny.'

'Mutiny!'

'Yes. I gather he was making a spirited attempt to persuade his entire section to desert to Moscow and join the Bolshevik revolution.'

'Ye gods, what a remarkable young man.'

'Yes. I think our masters realised it might not be politic to shoot him. If the story got out it might have started a few other corporals thinking along the same lines. Better to send him here and let it be known that he's gone mad. I'm sorry, Julius, that's not a word we use here, is it?'

36

'My dear David, you use whatever words you like.'

The tone was light, but I sensed that Dr Stroud disapproved of gossip about his patients' lives before they came to Nantgarrew. I suspected too that both Robin and David were, in their separate ways, seeing how far they could go with him, like children with an indulgent father. Which was ridiculous, because he and David must be much of an age.

The three of us parted in the hallway. David and Dr Stroud had decided to go to the kitchen in search of tea, but I wanted to change my damp skirt and dry my hair before breakfast. I lingered though at a notice-board in the hall where some official hand, almost certainly not Dr Stroud's, had pinned up Army Form C345, *Orders for Patients in Military and Auxiliary Hospitals*. Its general tone seemed to be that even if you were badly wounded, you needn't think the army was going to let go of you easily.

'Patients will obey the rules of the hospital. Patients marked "up" and "up, bed, down" will rise at the appointed hour, shave, wash and dress before breakfast.

Patients are not permitted to be in the hospital grounds after 5 pm in winter and sunset in summer.

Patients who are non-commissioned officers will assist the sisters and staff nurses or ward orderlies in maintaining good order and discipline.'

I noted that even if the unfortunate corporals and sergeants were confined to their beds they still had to display their stripes at the bed-head.

As I was going into my room the door next to it opened and Jenny looked out.

'Nell, what's happening?'

'Mrs Minter again. She came on a bicycle and hoisted a white flag.'

37

Jenny looked almost despairing at the news. If she'd slept, it didn't seem to have refreshed her.

'Please come in, Nell. Your hair's wet. What have you been doing?'

She didn't wait for an answer. 'What can we do about this dreadful woman?'

'Why not ignore her? Let her waste her time doing idiotic things if she wants to.'

'But it's so unfair and so dangerous.'

'Only if we're sure she fired the gun as well.'

'Dangerous to our work. You must speak to her, Nell.'

I promised to do that. I didn't tell her about David. I thought she might build too much on it.

Breakfast took place at two long tables in a dining-room overlooking the terrace and lawn. Somebody, probably the same person who'd pinned up *Orders for Patients*, had stuck posters over the walls. On one of them a crust of bread announced, 'When you throw me away or waste me you are adding twenty submarines to the German navy.' In spite of that, it looked a cheerful room and the half-dozen or so people sitting at the tables when I arrived might have been at a college rather than a hospital. One of them, a plump and cheerful-seeming man in his thirties, introduced himself as Dr Caspian. There were two nurses in blue dresses that were a compromise between uniform and informality, and a clergyman in a black suit and dog collar, referred to by the others as 'Padre'. I wasn't sure whether he was staff or patient until he looked at me and announced in a sonorous voice:

'To obey is better than sacrifice and to hearken than the fat of rams.'

Then he went back to his porridge.

It was my first chance to look for the two of Dr Stroud's patients I hadn't met so far. Stanley Gorton turned out to be a plump, prematurely balding man in his late thirties. His manner seemed placid, bumbling, but when I sat at the place beside him he had a way of looking at me sidelong, as if he suspected me of planning to steal the bacon from his plate. He wore glasses, a dark shirt of some

38

serviceable material and a pair of field glasses slung across his chest. He ate hugely. When he got up to help himself to more bacon and eggs, I noticed the limp. Apart from saying good morning he addressed just one question to me.

'Are you interested in raptors? I saw a female hen harrier yesterday.'

He gave no sign of knowing about Mrs Minter's latest raid and I decided not to raise the subject.

Soon afterwards Dr Stroud came in and engaged Stanley in what sounded like a knowledgeable conversation about birds of prey. Then the door opened again and standing there was the man who'd been watching me from the conservatory. Seen close to, he had the thin, tight-stretched skin that sometimes goes with aristocratic families at the end of their energies. He looked as if he'd meticulously obeyed the order to rise at the appointed hour, shave, wash and dress before breakfast. He stood in the doorway and said good morning to the room in general. Then he glanced at me, at Dr Stroud and raised an eyebrow. The request, or command, was clear and Dr Stroud obliged, though with an undercurrent of amusement in his voice.

'Miss Bray, may I introduce Ralph Keyson. Ralph, Miss Nell Bray.'

Keyson shook my hand coldly. I said: 'I notice you were up early too, Colonel Keyson.'

He made no answer to that, only asked if he could bring me more coffee. When he came back to the table with his cup and mine he said to Dr Stroud:

'I gather we had some unpleasantness again this morning.'

The remark, in an upper-class drawl, had the air of a senior officer asking a junior one for a report. Dr Stroud's reply was friendly enough, but firmly civilian.

'Another little demonstration. Hal and Robin saw her off with no great harm done.'

Since the subject had been opened I said to Colonel Keyson: 'Do you think it might have been Mrs Minter who fired at you in the conservatory?'

He gave me a look as if I'd mentioned politics in the mess.

'I've not the slightest idea.'

He went over to the serving table to help himself to porridge. Gorton gave him an anxious look then followed, carrying an empty plate. I was talking to Dr Stroud and didn't notice what was going on until I heard Stanley Gorton's voice, high and indignant.

'But there's plenty of toast. It will only go to waste.'

Keyson said something to him that I couldn't hear. Then Gorton's voice again.

'It's all very well for the King. He's not recovering from a war wound.'

It was clear what was happening. The month before His Majesty had signed a proclamation asking everybody to save food by eating less bread. Consumption in the royal household would be cut by at least a quarter and he hoped all his loyal subjects would follow the example. Stroud sighed, got up and walked over to them.

'What's the trouble, Stanley?'

'He says I can only have one slice of toast. There's plenty of toast. It will only . . .'

Keyson drawled: 'I was only suggesting a little self-restraint.'

The look Stroud gave him was suddenly a very professional one.

'I don't think self-restraint's necessary in this respect. We're not short of bread.'

Under Stroud's protection Gorton helped himself to three slices of toast and walked self-consciously back to the table with them. With Keyson's austere eye on him he smothered them with butter and marmalade and shovelled them down his throat in an untidy panic, all grease and crumbs. All the time, Keyson didn't take his eyes off him. When he'd finished, Gorton gave a great gulp and blinked, like a frog that had swallowed a fly. Keyson gave him one last look of disgust and turned away.

Dr Stroud said: 'If you'll all excuse me, I must go and deal with some forms. If anybody has any letters for posting, the boy will be going down to Cymyoy in half an hour. Stanley, your session is at half past nine, Robin at eleven. You,

Ralph, at midday.'

It was a reminder, probably deliberate, that we were a medical establishment.

As I left the dining room soon afterwards, Dr Stroud looked out of his study.

'Would you care to come in, Miss Bray? The forms can wait.'

It was a pleasant room, with no hint of the medical about it. A large bay window looked out onto the front lawn and the opposite slopes of the valley. There was a sturdy desk in dark wood, loaded with papers, a filing cabinet, several leather armchairs, a vase of irises and clove carnations on a small table, alongside a detailed model of a steam train. The only oddities were a couch covered with Turkish carpets and, on the wall above it, a photograph of a middle-aged man with a pointed beard.

'Dr Sigmund Freud, I presume.'

'That's right. Do sit down, Miss Bray. I shan't suggest that you lie down on my couch, at least not at this stage.'

He smiled and I found myself smiling back. Again, I had the impression of open air about him. He settled himself behind his desk as I thanked him for letting Jenny invite me.

'Jenny told me you were interested in Freudian psychology.'

'I hardly know enough about it to be interested. I gather there's something called the unconscious, which seems to be a logical impossibility.'

'Oh?'

'If you don't know about something, it doesn't exist for you. If you do know, then it's not unconscious.'

'Supposing that what you don't know is harming you because you don't know it.'

'It might harm you more if you did. Conscious life's quite complicated enough, without summoning up more complications.'

'But supposing a complicated way is the only one that takes you where you need to be.'

'In my experience there's usually a direct one to the same

41

place.'

He laughed. 'Dr Freud once referred to "the arrogance of the consciousness". I suspect that might describe your attitude, Miss Bray.'

He said it in a way that sounded neither hostile nor insulting.

'The reason that Jenny invited me was that she's worried about what's happening here and she hoped I might be able to do something about it.'

'Mrs Minter?'

'Yes, and that shot into the conservatory last Sunday. She thinks it might have been intended to kill somebody.'

'Do you believe that?'

'I've no opinion so far, but if it was intended to kill one of you, it seems a remarkably bad shot.'

'Yes?'

I was realising that it was a professional skill of his to turn the conversation back on me, so that I did most of the talking. Lawn tennis technique.

'Do you think it was intended to kill one of you?'

'Like you, I have no opinion. So far, at least.'

'If so, which one? Jenny thinks Stanley Gorton was the nearest.'

'Yes.'

'And Ralph Keyson the furthest away.'

'Yes.'

'With you in the middle?'

'Yes.'

'But I gather you'd only just opened the door when the shot was fired.'

'That's true.'

'So if the person was firing at you, he or she must have a very quick eye.'

'Yes, that would follow.'

'Yet he or she missed you by some yards.'

We stared at each other. I had the impression that he was taking this not quite seriously.

'You know Jenny thinks that either you or Ralph Keyson were the targets?'

'I do. She's insisted on discussing it with me several times.'

'Do you accept her theory that one of your patients might want to kill you because you remind him of his father?'

'That's a rather simplistic view of a transferred Oedipus Complex, but it's theoretically possible, yes.'

'Doesn't that worry you?'

'That would depend on whether I expected it to be repeated. I see no reason to expect that.'

'Doesn't that depend on who it was and what his motives were? Or hers?'

'Motives are a simple word for something very complicated.'

He was inviting me to walk down his road. I kept to mine.

'I gather you think the shot had nothing to do with Mrs Minter.'

'I didn't think I'd been so dogmatic. But we have no evidence so far of violent behaviour by the lady.'

'If it wasn't Mrs Minter, the assumption must be that it was somebody here at Nantgarrew.'

'I try very hard not to make assumptions.'

'Don't you want to know?'

'Only if it would be useful in treating an individual. Even then, it would probably only be useful if the individual decided to tell me about himself.'

I heard steps in the next room. Jenny put her head round the connecting door, saw me and hastily withdrew it.

'Miss Bray, may I ask you a question? Supposing you found out who fired that shot, what would you do about it?'

'Try to stop him or her doing it again.'

'How? Would you, for instance, inform the police or the War Office?'

'Only if it was essential.'

'I'd have to insist that you did not find it essential. Whatever happens, I'm not having my work here wrecked by ignorant and judgemental officials.'

'What if the aim's better next time?'

He smiled. 'Every one of my patients has risked his life, day after day, in some cases for two years or more. It doesn't seem much to ask that I should take a smaller risk.'

I found that hard to argue with, except on one point.

'One of them hasn't been risking his life. I don't suppose the casualty rate at divisional headquarters is very high.'

'Colonel Keyson, you mean? For a certain type of man, it might be worse sending other men to be killed than fighting in the trenches himself.'

'So Colonel Keyson eventually broke down under the strain?'

'That's not a concept I find useful. Everybody breaks down at some time.'

He had his elbows on the desk, chin in hands.

'Well, Miss Bray, do you accept my terms?'

'Terms?'

'If you stay here, there must be no question of reporting anybody to the authorities without consulting me.'

'I'm not in the habit of making terms for my visits, Dr Stroud.'

'Well, can we at least say that if you do discover something you'll discuss it with me before deciding what to do next?'

'Yes, I think that's fair enough.'

I stood up to go. He got up to see me to the door.

I said: 'By the way, what happened to the bullet?'

'Bullet?'

'The one that was found in the wall of the conservatory.'

'Oh, I think Ralph Keyson kept that. I don't know. I didn't give it much attention.'

He paused with his hand on the doorknob.

'I hope you enjoyed your swim this morning.'

I was almost dumbstruck.

'How did you know about that?'

'David Ellward told me when we were having our cup of tea together. Apparently he thought he was dreaming you. Quite an interesting development.'

I was angry, not so much because of my impulsive swim – though goodness knows that was embarrassing enough – but at everything else David must have told him to make sense of our meeting.

'Is it indeed? Well, when you're talking to Mr Ellward,

would you kindly tell him that I'm sorry to have trespassed on his unconscious.'

I banged the door behind me, feeling more than ready to deal with Monica Minter.

SIX

I FOUND JENNY IN A small office with a typewriter, next to Dr Stroud's room, and asked if I might borrow her bicycle.

'Yes, it's in the shed by the drive. But you'll need to take the pump. It's got a slow puncture.'

'Well, I can mend it.'

'Don't bother, the inner tube's just a mass of patches. I had a new one sent up from Abergavenny, but now it seems to have disappeared.'

I found the bicycle in the shed, also a folded sheet with tears down one side where the nails had gone, evidently Mrs Minter's white flag. I put that in the bicycle basket, pumped up the tyres and free-wheeled down the drive onto the road I'd trudged up the night before. I knew from the farmer that Mrs Minter was staying at the last house before the Cymyoy turning. It was easy to spot, a red brick house like a Victorian vicarage, picked out in contrasting patterns of black and yellow, sprouting prickly gables. It looked hot and uncomfortable among the green hills. As I swooped down the road I could see the bright red car parked on the gravel in front of it.

The front door opened as I was pedalling up the drive and Mrs Minter came out. She was wearing the brown cotton motoring coat unbuttoned over a brown suit of vaguely military cut, with above-ankle skirt and tight-waisted jacket, tricorn hat and red scarf as on the day before. Seen close to, she was a handsome woman in her thirties with a fine complexion and an easy, confident way of walking. If I'd met her in other circumstances I'd have instinctively liked her. Perhaps she felt the same, because when she saw me toiling up the last few yards of drive she smiled and came towards me. I laid the bike on its side and took out the white sheet.

'I've come to return your property.'

Her face changed.

'If you're from the cowards' rest home at Nantgarrew, take it back and tell them they can keep it. They've earned it.'

On the ride down I'd tried to forget my annoyance and promised myself that I'd be reasonably diplomatic, at least to begin with. I did my best.

'Mrs Minter, have you considered that you're being unfair? Those men are as badly wounded by the war as if they'd lost an arm or leg.'

'That strapping young man who chased me down the drive this morning didn't seem to have much wrong with him.'

'Mental suffering can be as bad as physical.'

(I hoped she'd never learn the details of young Robin's history.)

'Who decides that? Dr Stroud with his filthy German theories?'

'I might even share your doubts about Freudian psychoanalysis, but . . .'

'So-called Freudian psychoanalysis is no more than filth added to cowardice. It's no good trying to blind me with medical science. I know what goes on there.'

'From spying through windows, I suppose. I'm not trying to blind you with science. I'm just suggesting you try a little humanity.'

'I suppose you're one of the so-called medical staff who sit by the bedsides of these deserters asking them if they ever saw their mothers undressed.'

'You're wrong about that, too.'

But she was too wound up to take any notice.

'It's no use coming to me talking about mental suffering. My brother died at the head of his men on the first day of the Somme. Do you think he'd have complained about mental suffering? What would happen to the war if any

47

soldier whose courage was not equal to his duty thought he could get himself a soft bed at home by talking about mental suffering?'

By that point I'd decided that trying to be diplomatic was a waste of time.

'What else were you doing outside Dr Stroud's window this morning? There was something else besides the flag, wasn't there?'

A quick, hard smile.

'A little surprise for you all. Wait and see.'

'Was it you who fired the shot into the conservatory five days ago?'

I was sure that came as a shock to her. Up to then she'd been quite sure of her ground. Now she had to stop and think.

'Oh, so you're accusing me of that, are you?'

'Not accusing, asking.'

She hadn't needed to ask what I meant, but then the shooting had become a matter of local gossip.

'You wouldn't believe me whatever I told you, so there's no point in saying anything.'

'I might. I accept there's a difference between the hysterical schoolgirl tricks you've been playing so far and actually trying to kill somebody.'

I'd intended the 'hysterical schoolgirl' line to hurt and I could see that it did. It made her look at me closely for the first time. As she registered what she was seeing her whole manner changed. So far she'd been confident, now she was downright aggressive.

'I recognise you. You're the traitor Nell Bray. We were on the same platform once.'

'And on the same side.'

'You're the one who's changed sides. The true women of England are fighting to win the war, as they fought to win the Vote.'

'Some of us are fighting to end the war.'

'You're in the right place, aren't you, at Nantgarrew? Working underground for England's enemies, grubbing around like moles in the dirty secrets of people's minds.

Some of us prefer to protect our country.'

'And some of us prefer not to go round striking patriotic poses while men are coughing their lungs out in mud.'

We glared at each other, worlds apart. Goodness knows why Jenny had ever imagined I could do any good. I walked a few steps to leave the white sheet on the bonnet of her car, intending to bring an end to the conversation. When I turned round she was pointing a revolver at me.

It was a service revolver, standard issue. It's a heavy looking weapon but she was holding it at waist height and very steadily, like a woman who knew what to do with it. I glanced at it, then at her face, and took a step towards her so that we were only a few feet apart. In spite of the steadiness of the gun she was breathing faster than normal.

'You asked me if I'd fired a shot. This is a brave warrior's weapon. My brother's gun. It knows how to deal with traitors. If I have to use it, I shan't hesitate.'

We stared at each other. A sheep bleated from across the valley. Bees buzzed round the delphiniums in the border. I was still wondering what to say when I heard the front door opening and a voice behind me.

'Monica dear, I'm sorry to have kept you waiting.'

It was a bright and elderly voice, full of chintz sofas and small teacups. Mrs Minter slid the revolver back into the big pocket of her motoring coat.

'Don't worry, aunt, I've left plenty of time.'

I turned and saw a little grey-haired lady coming down the steps, wearing a lavender coloured dress and hat. She looked as if she'd stepped straight out of the reign of Queen Victoria without changing as much as a hairpin. When she saw me she gave a nervous little smile and obviously expected to be introduced, but Monica Minter just walked round me to open the passenger door for her, sweeping the white sheet off the bonnet of the car as she went. When they were both settled Mrs Minter tooted the horn and an elderly gardener appeared to crank up the car. She shouted at me over the noise:

'My aunt and I are going to a meeting of the Duty and

Discipline branch in Abergavenny. We shall be discussing how to support the men who are doing their duty.'

The engine came to life. She adjusted her goggles. Her aunt looked nervous, either of her niece or the prospect of a motor car journey, but she gave me a brave wave of the hand, stopping abruptly when Mrs Minter said something to her. They roared their way down the drive and by the time I'd cycled back down to the road they were almost out of sight, on their way to Abergavenny in a cloud of white dust.

Going in the opposite direction and hampered by the slow puncture, I pushed the bicycle up most of the two steep miles back to Nantgarrew. By the time I turned into the drive it was past eleven o'clock and the heat must have been up in the eighties. In spite of that, I saw that Dr Caspian had managed to get his half-dozen patients together for cricket practice in a field near the road. I wondered if Dr Freud had anything to say about cricket and decided not to ask. Stanley Gorton came limping down the drive towards me, his face pink and shiny with sweat.

'Ah Miss Bray, did you see the buzzards?'

He pointed to two birds wheeling over a field on the far side of the road.

'Can you hear them?'

I'd been conscious for some time of a distant mewing sound without realising it came from the birds.

'They're hunting. If you watch, you'll probably see one of them swoop. Unbelievable power.'

His small eyes glistened.

'Have you had your session with Dr Stroud?'

He nodded, looking embarrassed.

'Yes. I can't say I look forward to them. Seem to run out of things to talk about.'

'Do you tell him about your dreams?'

'They're always the same. Always about food. You know, stuck out there with only Maconochie army rations in tins and biscuits you wouldn't give a dog, you get into the habit of dreaming about food. Things like chump chops, brown

50

and crisp on the outside and running red when you cut into them. Fried eggs sizzling. And sausages.'

His eyes had a faraway look.

'The doctor said to me, "Describe your dream about sausages." Well, I ask you. I told him they were just sausages, raw and pink with that little puckering sound they make when cook pricks them, then all brown and shiny in the pan with the meat bursting out of the ends. As I said to him, just ordinary dreams about ordinary sausages.'

'Was he interested?'

'He seemed quite excited. Goodness knows why.'

'You don't sound very impressed with psychoanalysis.'

He snorted with laughter, spraying saliva.

'My dear lady, how would I know one way or the other? The only reason I'm here at all is because of the usual War Office cock . . . the usual War Office mix-up.'

'Mix-up?'

'At the hospital. There I was with a lump of shrapnel just dug out of my leg waiting to be sent to a convalescent home on the Isle of Wight. Somebody muddles up his signals so I end up in a loony bin in Wales instead.'

'Didn't you protest?'

'It's never any use protesting. That's the first thing you learn when they call you up. By the time they admit somebody's made a mistake the war will be over anyhow. Besides, the bird life's better here.'

He looked up again at the wheeling hawks.

'I gather you had a narrow escape in the conservatory last Sunday.'

He stared as if he didn't know what I was talking about.

'The shot.'

'Oh, that.' He looked embarrassed, as if it were some intimate personal ailment.

'It wasn't really anything to do with me, you know.'

'I thought it just missed you.'

'Yes, but it wasn't meant for me, was it? How could it have been?'

I remembered Jenny's description of how he'd been in a

state of hysteria. There was something eerie about his unconcern now.

'Does that mean you think it was meant for Dr Stroud or Ralph Keyson?'

'How would I know, dear lady? I wasn't the one who fired it, was I?'

'Who do you think fired it?'

He made a kind of neighing noise and fidgeted. He'd have liked to walk away from me, but the vestiges of manners forbade it.

'How would I know? Why should you think I'd know?'

'What happened exactly?'

'Hasn't Miss Chesney told you?'

'Yes, but I'd like to hear it from you. After all, she wasn't in the conservatory when it happened.'

He heaved a deep sigh and looked away from me over the valley.

'Colonel Keyson and I were having a conversation, then suddenly there was the sound of breaking glass and he shouted to me to get down.'

'How far away from him were you at the time?'

'About half the length of the conservatory. He was looking at one of those big geraniums, reckoned it had white-fly, as if that mattered to anybody.'

'Did you hear what direction the shot came from?'

'I didn't even hear the shot. The first I heard was the glass breaking.'

'What did Colonel Keyson do?'

'Nothing much.'

'Did he seem shaken?'

He made a face like a man sucking a lemon.

'You couldn't tell. He just stood there by the flower pot like a damned fool and went on talking about the bloody white-fly.'

'After you'd been shot at?'

'Yes. The doctor came rushing in asking what had happened. Keyson just stood there and said in that drawling voice of his that it appeared we'd been shot at and he really must get the garden boy to do something about the white-fly.'

I could just imagine Keyson saying it, and his public school affectation of unconcern.

'Then what?'

'Well, they all rushed outside to see if they could catch whoever it was. I couldn't go because of my leg.'

'And that was it?'

'That, as you say, was it, dear lady. Now if you'll excuse me . . .'

He went limping on down the drive.

I put the bike in the shed and went to look for Jenny, but as soon as I set foot in the porch I heard an argument going on inside the hall. Or at least, half an argument. The front door had been left ajar and I could hear the voice of Robin Duncan.

'I'm not lying there listening to you talking such bloody dirt. They can shoot me if they want to but I'm not taking this from any man, no matter who he is.'

Then the murmur of Dr Stroud's voice, calm and low. I couldn't hear the words. Then Jenny:

'Mr Duncan, please don't rush off like this.'

Dr Stroud, louder this time, but still calm: 'Let him go if he wants to, Miss Chesney.'

The front door was pushed fully open and Robin erupted from it. His face was as fiery as his hair.

'It's nothing but the stink from a rotten society, that's all it is.'

The words were thrown at me but he didn't seem to expect a reply. He rushed past me, across the lawn and over the bank in an angry, jerky run. He'd disappeared by the time Jenny and Dr Stroud came out.

I was curious to know what had caused the outburst but knew it was no good asking Dr Stroud about a patient. Instead I gave him and Jenny a report of my unsuccessful attempt at diplomacy with Mrs Minter. When I got to the revolver Jenny gasped, but Dr Stroud looked delighted and got me to repeat what she'd said.

'You see what I mean, Miss Chesney? This business of the weapon is a clear indication of both repressed incestuous attraction and penis envy towards her late brother. Combined, I suspect, with a strong guilt complex. I should love to get that woman on my couch.'

'I wish she were a lot further away than that.'

Jenny seemed cast down by my failure to make Mrs Minter see reason, but Dr Stroud refused to be disturbed either by that or Robin's outburst. He suggested to her that she should go and look for Ralph Keyson and let him know that he could bring his appointment forward by half an hour.

Jenny thought she'd seen him going down the drive some time before. As we strolled down together I asked her what had upset Robin so much.

'Something Dr Stroud asked him about his childhood.'

'I guessed that.'

'Robin's a person who is threatened by his unconscious. He spends a lot of his energy trying to deny what it's telling him. That's why he's so tense and angry.'

'Of course he's angry. He's a revolutionary.'

'Repression often takes the form of extreme political beliefs.'

'Or sausages?'

Jenny looked at me anxiously, as if she thought I'd been affected by the sun.

'I had a talk with Stanley Gorton. Apparently the only thing he dreams about is food. But since he's here on false pretences, I don't suppose it matters.'

'False pretences?'

Now she was alarmed. I told her what Stanley Gorton had said about the War Office and she took it as bad news.

'Nell, you really mustn't believe what Stanley Gorton tells you. I can't tell you all I know about him, but believe me, Stanley Gorton was not sent here by mistake.'

'But he has a leg wound.'

'The leg wound's the least of it.'

She bit her lip and wouldn't say any more. We turned a bend in the drive and saw Ralph Keyson standing by the gate post. He was watching Stanley Gorton, who in turn was watching the buzzards through his field glasses, leaning over a wall about fifty yards up the road. A thin burst of applause from the field next to us suggested that one of Dr Caspian's cricketing squad had made a good catch.

Jenny delivered Dr Stroud's message and the three of us walked back together up the drive. We talked about the weather and the buzzards, but I noticed that Keyson's rather old-fashioned courtesy seemed even more marked when he was with Jenny and that he looked at her intently when she spoke, as if her slightest word mattered. Jenny seemed aware of it too and the heightened colour of her cheeks wasn't due to the sun. I wondered if the conversation might have been different if I hadn't been there. Dr Stroud was waiting for us on the steps. We left Ralph Keyson with him and I suggested to Jenny that we might stay out on the lawn for a while because there were several things I needed to ask her. Reluctantly, she let herself be guided away from the house.

'I've got a pile of notes to type up for Dr Stroud's book. We've been getting terribly behind-hand with them.'

'Is he using . . .?'

I felt the explosion a split second before I heard it, a kind of punch on the air. Then the crash of sound, the whole valley ringing with it, and a spurt of glass fragments flying out from the window of Dr Stroud's study. After that there was a moment of total silence then Jenny said:

'Oh God, not again.'

She was close behind me as I ran into the house.

SEVEN

THE DOOR OF DR STROUD'S study was open and a smell of explosives came from inside. Dr Stroud and Colonel Keyson were standing just outside the door, looking into the room. The whole wall facing us, the one with the couch and the picture of Dr Freud, was virtually wrecked. The couch itself, with both legs shattered at one end, had collapsed like a shot animal, the rugs from it ripped and thrown round the room. The wall above it was pockmarked with holes, the plaster dust from them still eddying in beams of sun from the shattered window. The carpet was ripped and scored in hundreds of places and chairs bulging with escaping stuffing. Jenny let out a sob.

'What happened?'

Ralph Keyson said: 'There appears to have been an explosion.'

His superior drawl sounded quite as usual. He was looking at the wrecked room as if it were mildly interesting. Dr Stroud was blinking quickly, but apart from that he seemed almost as calm. When I asked if anybody was hurt he was the one who replied.

'Fortunately not. Ralph and I were just on our way in when it happened. Luckily, we were still on the outside of the door.'

Keyson took a few steps into the room and bent down.

'Be careful,' Jenny said.

He ignored her, and picked up a piece of metal.

'A hand grenade. Careful, it's still hot.'

Dr Stroud took the jagged fragment and looked at it

carefully, then knelt down by the couch.

'Yes indeed. There are more pieces of it here. It rather looks as if it scored a direct hit on the couch.'

'Oh, do be careful both of you. There's glass all over the place.'

Jenny was right. The photograph of Dr Freud was staring at us from the carpet, almost unharmed, but the glass from it was scattered in fragments all round. In the way that so many people have of occupying themselves with details in a crisis, Jenny went for the picture. It was coming away from its frame so she bundled it up in a piece of torn rug. Meanwhile Dr Stroud and Ralph Keyson, preoccupied as boys hunting shells, went on collecting pieces of grenade.

I said: 'Where did it come from?'

'A good question. Jenny, what about the records? Is the cabinet all right?'

Jenny propped Dr Freud against the wall and went across to the cabinet by the desk. It had gone piebald coloured, with streaks of light wood showing against the dark varnish, but looked undamaged apart from that. 'I think it's all right. Shall I check?'

She opened it with a key from her pocket and began to check through the files.

'Yes, it seems to be all right, thank God.'

'Yes, the rest can be replaced, even our poor couch. I'm afraid we're going to have to postpone your session, Ralph – unless you fancy a bench in the garden.'

Calm was all very well, but this seemed to me too much of a good thing. I sensed that Dr Stroud felt challenged by Colonel Keyson's ostentatious lack of panic and was determined to equal it. I was about to repeat my question when we heard Captain Hunter's voice from the hall.

'This way, sergeant. It's the doctor's study.'

The two of them burst in on us. At least, with Captain Hunter around, there was no further danger of an overdose of calm. He came through the doorway as if he expected to deal with a German raiding party inside, closely followed by Jack Kelso.

'What's happening?'

Dr Stroud got in first. 'As you can see, Hal, somebody seems to be playing silly tricks with a hand grenade.'

'Where did it come from?'

This time Hal Hunter and I spoke at once. He glared at me.

'We don't know.'

Jack Kelso had been saying nothing but using his eyes.

'Through the window would be the most likely place, Sir. Did you see anything?'

'No. Nobody was in the room at the time. Colonel Keyson and myself would have been in a couple of seconds.'

'You were lucky, Sir.'

'Yes. In fact, somebody did us a favour without meaning to, didn't he, Ralph?'

He laughed. Ralph Keyson's calm gave way to a look of embarrassment.

'I'm quite sure that wasn't the effect intended.'

'Of course not. A simple adolescent regression to defying quasi-parental authority. Still, it had its uses.'

'What happened?'

Dr Stroud turned to me.

'I actually had my hand on the doorknob when Ralph drew my attention to the notice about orders for patients in military hospitals. Brigadier Moss made us put it up in the hall.'

'Yes, I'd noticed. What about it?'

'Ralph had just noticed that somebody had made an unauthorised addition to it. He may tell you what it was, if you ask him.'

Keyson scowled.

'It's hardly a word I can say in front of ladies, is it?'

'As you like. Anyway, there I was just about to push the door open when Ralph pointed this out to me. If I hadn't stopped to glance at it . . .'

He looked round the room and shrugged. Jenny shivered and turned back to her files.

Jack Kelso went over to the window, crunching on glass.

'I see it's propped halfway open, Sir. Did you leave it like that?'

'Yes. It was hot in here. I opened the window and left the door ajar when I went out, to get a current of air through.'

'That's it, then, Sir. Somebody stood outside on the flower bed and threw it in through the window.'

Hal Hunter said: 'If she came up the drive, I don't see how we could have missed seeing her.'

'We might have, you know, Sir. We weren't looking that way much of the time.'

I asked: 'What were you doing?'

'Measuring up for the next lot of wire, Miss.'

With Captain Hunter there the reply was deadpan, as if their unfinished barbed wire fence was a perfectly reasonable job of work.

Hunter said stubbornly: 'We'd have seen her.'

I said: 'If you're thinking about Mrs Minter, I don't see how it could have been her this time. It's only just over an hour since I saw her driving off towards Abergavenny.'

'She could easily have driven back again.'

Hunter glared at me.

'Yes, but she'd have had to pass me on the road. And if she'd driven up this way after I got back, Colonel Keyson would have seen her. He was down at the bottom of the drive.'

'The Colonel didn't stay at the bottom of the drive though, did he? He was up here with Dr Stroud.'

'Are you saying we shouldn't have heard a motor car in a quiet place like this?'

'She didn't have to come all the way in her motor car. She could have parked it down the valley and walked across the fields. That would explain why Sergeant Kelso and I didn't see her.'

'But there were Dr Caspian and his cricketers down in the field next to the drive. She'd have had to get past them as well.'

He said stubbornly: 'Well, she must have managed it somehow.'

It seemed that for Hal Hunter Mrs Minter possessed supernatural powers, able to be in two places at once and make herself invisible.

Jenny, still checking files, suddenly joined the conversation.

'Nell, wouldn't we have seen somebody by the window? We were out there, after all.'

I thought about it.

'Not necessarily. We'd only just set foot on the lawn when the explosion happened, and after that all we thought about was coming to see what had happened. If there'd been somebody lying low in the flower bed we might have missed him.'

'Or her.'

That came from Captain Hunter.

While all this was going on Dr Stroud had been strolling round the room, ruefully looking at his wrecked possessions. He apparently decided that the discussion had gone on long enough.

'I don't think there's a lot we can do here. The others will have to know about it, of course, but I suggest we make as little of it as possible. Luckily, nobody's actually been hurt.'

'But you can't just wait for them to do it again.'

Jenny's protest brought her a warning look from Dr Stroud, as if it was none of her business. Captain Hunter supported her.

'Yes, the question is, what are we going to do about defending ourselves? I've shown you my rota for patrols. If we take it in turns, two men on four hour watches . . .'

'Hal, I'm not converting the whole of Nantgarrew into a fortified camp because of a few malicious incidents. As I say, nobody's been hurt.'

'Not yet. Are we supposed to sit here like a covey of pacifists until somebody gets killed?'

Keyson murmured: 'Easy, Captain, easy.'

Hal looked round the half-circle of us, keeping a special glare for me. Then he turned on his heel and marched out. Jack Kelso looked at Dr Stroud, was given a nod, and followed him at an easier pace.

Ralph Keyson drawled: 'See you at lunch then, doctor. Let me know if I can do anything.'

Then he too left with a last glance at the wrecked couch.

As soon as he was gone, Jenny tried to start tidying up, but Dr Stroud stopped her.

'Not yet. You need time to recover from the shock.'

'I'm all right.'

'No you're not. Miss Bray, will you kindly take her out for a walk on the lawn?'

As we got out to the porch Dr Caspian came panting up, wanting to know what had happened. Jenny told him.

'Oh God. We heard the bang. I told my people to stay down in the field out of the way while I came up and found out what was going on.'

I asked him if he'd seen anything out of the ordinary. The question seemed to puzzle him.

'Before the bang, you mean? No.'

'Or after it?'

'No.'

'Were all your six patients down in the field with you when it happened?'

'Yes. One batting, one bowling and four fielding, if you count the padre. What shall I do about them?'

Jenny, keeping a tight hold on herself, said sensibly that they might as well go on playing cricket. He thought about it, nodded and went running off.

I walked Jenny to the bench on the terrace and made her sit down. She was almost crying with anger.

'Why won't he do something? Why won't somebody do something?'

'Will he tell the police now, do you think?'

She shook her head.

'Nell, was it that woman?'

'I don't honestly see how it could have been.'

'It's so hard to accept after all that anybody hates him so much that they want to kill him.'

'But it's odd, isn't it? Whoever threw that grenade couldn't have seen who it was on the other side of the door.'

'They'd know who was going in there.'

'Would they, though? Remember, we were the only two who knew Ralph Keyson's appointment had been brought forward by half an hour.'

'Could it have been somebody deliberately throwing it into an empty room?'

'Yes, in which case it could be madness or malice, rather than a wish to kill. Dangerous malice, though.'

She was silent, watching Dr Caspian trotting back to his cricketers.

'Nell, are you thinking what I'm thinking?'

'Robin Duncan?'

She nodded.

'Yes, if there's one person we know was ready to hurl a grenade at Dr Stroud's couch, it's Robin Duncan. I wonder where he was at the time.'

'So you think it was him?'

'I don't know. Let's look at this by a process of elimination. Somebody must have thrown that grenade. It wasn't you, or me or Ralph Keyson or Dr Stroud. Can we take it that Dr Caspian's right about all his patients being with him at the time?'

'Oh yes. It's not just a game of cricket, you see. He's working on a thesis about neurosis and physical co-ordination, so he'd be watching them and making notes.'

'Well, that seems to rule out another six, plus Dr Caspian himself. And although it's theoretically possible that the cook or the gardening boy took a few minutes off work and threw it, I suppose we can rule out the domestic staff for the time being.'

'Yes.'

'So who's left?'

I waited for her answer. It came reluctantly.

'Dr Stroud's other patients.'

'Yes. Five other patients: Hal Hunter, Jack Kelso, Stanley Gorton, Robin Duncan and David Ellward.'

She glanced at me when I said the last name and I knew she'd learned somehow about our old friendship. It was probably in the case notes already.

I said: 'And I think we can rule out one of those five, provisionally at any rate.'

Another glance.

'Who?'

'Stanley Gorton.'

'Oh.'

She was disappointed.

'You remember that we saw him some distance up the road, watching buzzards. It's just possible that he might have got back in time to throw the grenade, but unlikely. He's fat and he limps. Also, he couldn't have fired that shot into the conservatory because he was there at the time, and I think we have to assume that the same person was responsible for both.'

'Yes.'

'So that leaves four. Of those, we know that Hal Hunter and Jack Kelso weren't far away at the time. We don't know where David Ellward or Robin Duncan were, but Robin couldn't have been far away either. And he was a very angry young man.'

'But Nell, I explained to you, anger's often a necessary stage in psychoanalysis.'

'For all we know, throwing hand grenades may turn out to be a necessary stage in psychoanalysis too. It's an infant science after all.'

Hurt silence.

Perhaps I shouldn't have said what came into my mind during the silence. It was unformed, hardly an idea at all.

'Of course, all this assumes that the grenade was thrown.'

'Of course it was. How else would it get into the room?'

'Supposing it was there all the time? Supposing it had been lodged on the couch, waiting for somebody to lie down on it?'

She stared at me, mouth open.

'Nell, that's an awful idea.'

'Dr Stroud announced at breakfast when he'd be seeing people. It was Stanley Gorton first. Did he lie down on the couch?'

'Yes, of course he did.'

'Then Robin Duncan, but he's lighter than Stanley so . . .'

'But Nell, he didn't. He refused to lie down on the couch at all.'

'Did he? That's interesting.'

'Why? Do you think he knew . . .?'

'I don't think anything yet. So the next person on the couch would have been Ralph Keyson?'

'Yes.'

It was almost a whisper.

'Except it went off before he could get there. Tell me about this couch business, Jenny. Do people just come in and lie straight down on it?'

'More or less. It depends, but . . . yes.'

'So Dr Stroud sits at his desk and makes notes while . . .'

'No. That's too remote. The analyst sits on a chair by the head of the couch.'

'Close to it?'

'Of course.'

I pictured the wrecked couch, the torn carpets, the pitted wall. If Dr Stroud had been sitting by it he, as much as Colonel Keyson, could have been the likely target.

A maid in a kitchen apron came running across the lawn towards us. Jenny tensed, expecting more trouble.

'Miss Chesney, the cook's gone under the table and won't come out. When she heard the bang she thought it was the Germans come for us.'

Her eyes were wide and scared. Jenny took control.

'It's all right, Megan. It's just another silly accident. Nobody's been hurt. I'll come and talk to the cook.'

They went off together. It was nearly two o'clock before the bell rang for lunch. On the way in I paused at *Orders for Patients in Military and Auxiliary Hospitals* to see the unauthorised addition that might have saved the lives of Dr Stroud and Colonel Keyson. It was scrawled across the notice in red wax crayon. 'Bollocks', it said.

EIGHT

DAVID DIDN'T COME IN TO lunch and nobody seemed to know where he was. Dr Stroud made an announcement over the cold beef salad.

'In case anybody hasn't heard yet, I should tell you there was an occurrence in my study a little while ago. Nobody was hurt. I suggest we don't gossip about it to outsiders.'

I could guess that meant Brigadier Moss or anybody from the War Office. There were only two people at lunch who might not have known what had happened, Stanley Gorton and Robin Duncan. Robin went on eating stolidly, as if he hadn't heard. Stanley, who'd managed to take a double helping of beef, paused with a forkful on the way to his mouth.

'What sort of occurrence?'

Hal Hunter said impatiently: 'A grenade. You must have heard it.'

'A grenade? I heard . . . I thought . . .'

There was sweat on his forehead. He looked ready to burst into tears.

Dr Stroud said gently: 'You heard it, but you thought you were imagining it?'

Stanley Gorton nodded several times, very quickly, then started forking in food in great mouthfuls, swallowing in painful, retching gulps. Then he began coughing and the tears came. Dr Stroud took him gently by the arm and led him out of the room.

After the meal, which was mostly silent, Robin Duncan tried to slip away without speaking to anybody. I followed him out to the lawn and caught up with him as he stood looking at the broken windows of the study.

I said: 'It was more of a gesture than a deliberate attempt to kill somebody, don't you think?'

He turned round to me, looking both angry and miserable and hardly old enough to be out of school.

'I wouldn't know about that.'

'Nobody was inside the room at the time.'

He made no comment.

'Did you hear it?'

He nodded.

'You didn't come to see what had happened.'

'You soon get out of the habit of running to look every time you hear a grenade going off.'

'But this isn't the trenches.'

He gave me a long look.

'Everywhere's the trenches.'

'Where were you when you heard it?'

'Over there.'

He glanced at the field next door.

'Doing what?'

'Lying down in the grass and thinking. Have I got permission to think?'

'Did you see anyone?'

'Why do you want to know?'

'Aren't you interested in who threw it?'

'No. Are you?'

'Yes.'

'Why?'

'Because somebody might get killed next time.'

He made a derisive noise.

'Do you know how many people were killed and injured on the Somme? Nearly half a million.'

'Yes, I know. But what's that got to do with it?'

'It's got bloody everything to do with it. There's men getting killed in their hundreds of thousands, and you expect me to be worried because one might get killed here.'

'If we stop caring about one life, then we stop caring about the hundreds of thousands. An individual life's got to matter, or the war's beaten all of us.'

66

It mattered to me very much to convince him. His face stayed angry and stubborn.

'One life doesn't matter. It's only the life of a whole class that matters, the class that's going to make a world where this won't happen again. Compared to that, I don't give a fart for what happens to anybody in this place. Or to me either.'

'I gather you don't approve of Freudian psychoanalysis.'

'It's no more than an excuse for the so-called intellectual classes to make dirty talk.'

'The grenade blew up Dr Stroud's couch.'

'Is that so.'

'Did you throw it?'

'I did not.'

His face and voice were impassive.

'Did you write "Bollocks" on the *Order for Patients*?'

'I did not. Now is that all of your questions? If it is, I've got better things to think about.'

I watched him striding away across the lawn and decided it was time to find somebody else on the short list.

The sun had shifted past its highest point but was still beating down as I climbed over the stile in the wall near the waterfall and followed a sheep track slanting up the steep field to the right of the house. When Nantgarrew was a long way below me I stopped and looked back. I could see the boy raking the lawn and from somewhere below him I heard the tap of a hammer. Probably Hal Hunter and Jack Kelso working on the wire again. Jenny was just outside the front door, deep in conversation with Dr Caspian. Apart from that nothing stirred in the grounds of Nantgarrew or up and down the valley road.

As I climbed higher and came to where waves of bracken met, the pasture flies buzzed round me. I flapped at them with my hat. A voice said, only a few feet away from me:

'That's no good, Nell. It only encourages them.'

I jumped higher than a mountain goat.

'David! Of all the . . . '

He was lying resting on his elbow in a little grassy space between two patches of bracken.

'You still walk with a swing, Nell. It was like the old days in the Alps, watching you.'

'Have you been up here all day?'

'Round and about.'

'Did you know somebody nearly killed Dr Stroud and Colonel Keyson with a grenade?'

He seemed no more than politely interested.

'I thought I heard something about midday. Did they get the right one?'

'As it happened, the only casualty was a picture of Dr Freud.'

'A pity.'

He might have meant the picture, but I thought not.

'Even supposing somebody hated Ralph Keyson enough to want to kill him, it would have been an act of madness to risk killing Dr Stroud as well.'

I watched his face. It didn't change.

'But we are mad, Nell. That's why we're here.'

I sat down on the grass beside him.

'Where were you when you heard it?'

'Am I a suspect? How interesting.'

'Co-operate then. Where were you?'

Without turning round, he pointed uphill.

'There's a path that runs all the way along the top of the ridge.'

'Can you see Nantgarrew from it?'

'Parts of it. In some stretches the path goes right along the edge. In others you have higher ground between you and the valley. You'd have to climb up a few feet.'

'When you heard it, it didn't occur to you to step up a few feet and see what was happening?'

He shook his head.

'Are you like Robin Duncan, not even interested when a grenade goes off?'

'If I thought about it at all, I must have thought it was blasting from the quarry.'

'If you're expecting me to believe that you can't tell the difference between a grenade and quarry blasting, I don't.'

'You always were a sceptical woman, Nell.'

There was a clump of harebells by our feet, the colour of the sky.

'Shall we leave them all to get on with it, Nell? Buy a cottage in the hills here, play music and live on bread and goat cheese?'

'You must have looked down on Nantgarrew sometimes. What did you see?'

He sighed. 'I saw Stanley Gorton limping up the road. I saw Colonel Ralph Keyson giving the valley the benefit of his inspection from the bottom of the drive. I saw Dr Caspian and his party playing rounders.'

'It was meant to be cricket.'

'It looked like rounders.'

'You didn't happen to see Monica Minter walking across the fields, I suppose?'

He laughed.

'With a bunch of white feathers in one hand and a grenade in the other? No. Is she a suspect?'

'Not a promising one, although Captain Hunter is convinced she did it.'

'Hal Hunter's a bit of a fool. Perhaps he threw it himself.'

'In fact, he was one of the first on the scene. But he and Jack Kelso give each other an alibi.'

David laughed again.

'I'm sorry, Nell, you can't help it. You've never been in the trenches. You know Jacko was a platoon sergeant in the company Hal Hunter commanded? They went through the Somme together. Jacko saved Hunter's life, stayed with him under fire in a shell crater in no-man's land all night, kept him from slipping into the mud and drowning. They gave Jacko the Military Medal for that.'

'I didn't know that.'

I watched a striped caterpillar hunching its way along a bracken stem.

'So what you're telling me is that Hal Hunter and Jack Kelso would back each other up?'

'Against the devil and all his dominions if necessary.'

'Do they hate Ralph Keyson enough to throw a grenade at him?'

'As much as I do. We were all in the same division, and he's a divisional staff officer. They've seen friends killed because of that bastard, just as I have.'

'But there must have been a crowd of staff officers at headquarters. Was he so much worse than the rest?'

'Yes. What you must understand, Nell, is that Keyson wasn't your usual fat, idle, red-tabbed incompetent of a staff officer. He was much worse. He's an ambitious devil and it was an open secret that the general let him try his hand at some of the smaller attack plans. We could tell them a mile off. Whenever we were given orders for an operation that looked elegant on paper but would be bloody carnage for the people who had to carry it out, you could bet Keyson was the man behind it.'

'But in the end it caught up with him. That's why he's here.'

'God knows what he's doing here. In hell is where he should be. If I took a truck full of grenades into Piccadilly and hurled them in all directions, I still shouldn't manage to kill as many people on our own side as he has.'

I said: 'Were you responsible for that grenade this morning?'

He smiled and closed his eyes.

I sat beside him and listened to the insects buzzing. It was several minutes before he spoke again, and then he didn't answer my question.

'So Dr Stroud's trying to make you believe Keyson's a penitent character, is he?'

'Jenny seems to think so.'

He snorted. I carried on.

'There's certainly something odd about the man. Very early this morning, before you saw me, he was standing there in the conservatory, staring out.'

'At you?'

'It looked like it.'

'What were you doing at the time?'

'Trying to get the scene of that shooting clear in my

70

mind.'

'That being why Jenny summoned you?'

'Yes.'

'She shouldn't have done it. She should have left well alone.'

His eyes were still closed.

I said: 'I'm afraid Jenny may be in love with Ralph Keyson.'

His eyes opened.

'What makes you think that?'

'Her worry, a nervousness when she talks about him, a tension when they're together. Had you noticed?'

'No. Women's work.'

'I don't think she'll admit it to me. She knows how you feel about him.'

'It's no secret. Well, if she is, God help the girl.'

He tipped his hat over his eyes. I sat looking over the valley.

'You know, David, if somebody was trying to kill Colonel Keyson it was a clumsy attempt, both times.'

'But I could never throw a cricket ball straight, could I? Don't you remember?'

I remembered. I stood up, brushed grass off my skirt and picked up my hat. David still had his over his eyes and gave no sign of noticing as I walked away downhill. When I looked up, all I could see of him were two tweed knees sticking up above the bracken.

NINE

TEA WAS SERVED ON THE lawn, big brown pots and plates of currant bread put out for people to help themselves. Dr Stroud strolled up to me with his teacup as I was looking at the trampled flower bed outside his study. The efforts of the gardening boy, making temporary repairs to the windows, had obliterated any traces that might have been left by somebody standing there to throw a grenade.

'Have you by any chance seen David Ellward? He was due for a session with me an hour ago. I've taken over Miss Chesney's office.'

'Didn't he turn up? I'm sorry.' Then I was angry with myself for feeling the need to apologise for him. 'Yes, I met him up there on the hill. He's been walking again.'

Dr Stroud looked tired, which wasn't surprising. After the two crises of the morning he'd spent his afternoon calming Stanley and waiting vainly for David. I asked him if he'd reported the grenade to anybody and discovered he hadn't.

Afterwards I looked for Jack Kelso and found him helping Megan to collect up the teacups. He was as friendly as ever, with no sign of whatever neurosis it was that had brought him to Nantgarrew. He mentioned, with no apparent concern, that he was due to give Dr Stroud his dream report at six o'clock.

'Dream report, is that what you call it?'

'That's it. Out on patrol over your dreams every night, report in full to the doctor every day.'

'Do you have many dreams for him?'

He shook his head.

'Only the usual ones. I'm there in the shell hole with a line of Huns coming at me. I know I've got my rifle and bayonet somewhere, but I can't see them. I'm feeling for them in the mud, but I can't get at them. I wake up sweating cobs with those Huns coming at me and no rifle, night after bloody night. Excuse the language, Miss.'

His voice was even and he told it almost as if it were a joke, but his hands were shaking.

'You saved Captain Hunter's life, didn't you?'

'He had a bad time.'

We walked together to the house and into the comparative coolness of the hall. It seemed cruel to probe any further, but it had to be done.

'I gather Colonel Keyson was on your divisional staff.'

'That's right. Not that I had anything to do with him personally. Sergeants don't have dealings with the Red Tabs – apart from being on the receiving end of their bright ideas.'

I said, as suddenly as the idea came into my head: 'Where would anybody round here get his hands on a grenade?'

I don't know what I'd expected – shock, blankness, anger. What I wasn't prepared for was the reaction I got. Jack Kelso stood still, then a slow smile spread over his face.

'Well, Miss, that's very interesting you should ask. Would you like to come upstairs and take a look at something?'

I followed him upstairs. He paused on the landing.

'I wouldn't normally take the liberty of inviting a lady into my room, but in the circumstances . . .'

He led me to a door at the far end, paused before opening it to check that there was nobody else about, and stood aside to let me in.

'I have to double up with that young Bolshevik, but he's still out of the way downstairs.'

It was a room much like my own, two beds with patchwork quilts, two narrow wardrobes, one chair and curtains pulled back to let the sun stream in, all of it meticulously tidy.

'Sit down, Miss. Now I know you won't go talking to the rest of them about this, but Miss Chesney told me about you going down and having a barney with that madwoman. I don't blame you for wanting something to defend yourself with. Not that a grenade's what I'd recommend. Still, if it's a grenade you fancy . . .'

I sat speechless, trying to find words to explain the misunderstanding. Jack Kelso had bent down and was dragging something heavy out from under his bed. It was a narrow brown painted wooden box with rope handles. An ammunition box.

'Mr Kelso, I . . .'

He glanced up at me, put a finger to his lips and undid a strap round the box.

'Don't worry, Miss, they're quite safe as long as you know how to handle them.'

He opened the lid.

I'd never seen a box of grenades before. Sitting there with their red painted tops they looked obscenely like a clutch of Easter eggs. He picked one of them out and handed it to me. I nearly dropped it from surprise and the weight of it. It was marked with deeply indented squares, like a small pineapple made of cast iron, with a metal lever down the side. I managed to stop my hand just before the thing hit my leg and sat there clutching it, waiting for the bang.

'Don't worry, Miss. It scares everybody for the first time. It can't explode unless you take that out from there.'

He touched a thin horizontal rod that ran across the neck of the grenade with a ring hanging from it.

'Then for goodness sake don't take it out.'

And I'd thought he was the sane one. I remembered his expression, 'sweating cobs'. It was what I was doing myself.

'I'm not going to. But even if I did it wouldn't matter as long as you held down that lever at the side. As long as that's down it won't go off, even with the pin out. Then, when you throw it . . .'

He stood up, holding an imaginary grenade against his chest with his right hand, left finger hooked into the ring of the pin, mimed a throwing action with his right arm.

'. . . you have to let go of the lever then, of course. Once

74

you do that, you've got five seconds.'

An expressive upward movement with his hands described what happened after that. I looked at the corrugated egg in my hand and tried not to shudder.

'You know, some of the lads use them as booby traps. Say we had to leave a trench and we knew the Huns were coming to take it, you could take the pin out and wedge it somewhere – in between two lots of duckboards, say – with the lever held in. Then as soon as somebody stepped on the duckboards it would topple over, up would go the lever and . . . there you are.'

Or aren't, as the case may be. The cold thing was becoming hot from the grip of my hand.

'But you wouldn't want to carry one of those round in your pocket all the time, would you, Miss?'

'No, I certainly would not.'

I tried, gingerly, to hand the thing back to him, but he went down on his knees again and started pulling out another box from under the bed.

'Now what I suggest is, I lend you one of these.'

He took out something wrapped in a clean duster. He twitched the duster off and there was an officer's service revolver, much like the one I'd seen a few hours ago in Mrs Minter's hand.

'You could carry this one around in your bag, or your pocket if it's big enough.'

I found my voice.

'Mr Kelso, it's very kind of you, but I don't want a revolver. I don't want a grenade either. I was just curious, that's all.'

Still holding the revolver, he grinned up at me from the floor.

'You needn't be afraid, Miss. They're quite safe. These don't go off accidentally.'

'I'm not afraid.' A lie, of course. 'But I don't think I need a grenade or a revolver to protect myself against Mrs Minter.'

At that moment I felt what I needed was somebody to protect me against Sergeant Jack Kelso. But he seemed so mild, so friendly, sitting there with his treasures on the rug by the bed.

'Oh well, if you change your mind you'll know where to come. Only don't tell the others or they'll all be wanting one.'

To my relief he took the grenade from me.

'What else have you got there?'

'Another revolver like this one and a Luger from a German officer. Then there's a couple of spare bayonets, some field glasses and a German stick bomb that came into our dug-out and didn't explode. I keep those in the wardrobe.'

He said it as if it were the most natural thing in the world.

'But where did you get them?'

He winked.

'Ways and means. You never know what you're going to need, do you?'

I waited until he'd wrapped up the revolver and tucked the grenade away with the rest. Then, making sure I had a clear path to the door, I said:

'Was it one of your grenades that was thrown this morning?'

He stood up, twitching at the knees of his trousers to shake out the creases.

'It could have been.'

'Could have been?'

'Somebody took a couple of mine three or four days ago. There should have been a dozen in that box. I don't know if you noticed, but there were only ten.'

'Have you any idea who took them?'

He shook his head.

'Did you tell Dr Stroud?'

'With respect, Miss, you get out of the habit of that kind of thing in the trenches. You didn't steal kit from a man in your own section, but apart from that anything you could lay your hands on was fair game. No good complaining to the officers if you lost something and making trouble. You just went and took a replacement from the unit next door when you got the chance.'

76

Goodness knows how he'd managed to bring his private armoury to Nantgarrew with him.

'Don't you lock your room?'

'The doctor doesn't allow locks.'

'Who would have known about them?'

'People find out.'

'Captain Hunter knew?'

'Oh yes.'

'And Robin Duncan must know.'

He shrugged. 'He minds his business and I mind mine.'

He seemed quite unaware of the significance of what he'd been saying. I tried another tack.

'You said it would be five seconds from when you let go of the lever to when it went off. Could it be longer than that?'

It was still in my mind that somebody might have planted the grenade under the couch earlier in the day, timed to explode during Colonel Keyson's session. If Jack guessed what I was thinking, he gave no sign of it.

'Some of them can be as long as seven seconds. It depends on the length of the fuse inside.'

'No longer than that?'

'No, seven seconds is about the limit I've heard of. There's no room in a grenade for much more fuse than that.'

Even if Jack was playing a double game, he'd hardly lie about something that could be checked so easily. Reluctantly I abandoned my theory of a timed explosion. I complimented Jack on his collection. I thanked him for his kind offer of a loan from it. He showed me out, his politeness and cheerfulness unimpaired.

Before dinner I went to see Dr Stroud at his temporary quarters in Jenny's study. I didn't like to betray Jack Kelso's hoard but couldn't think of any safe alternative.

'Dr Stroud, are you aware that Jack Kelso keeps a box of hand grenades and three guns under his bed?'

He nodded.

'It seems quite a reasonable precaution.'

'Reasonable! I suppose he's keeping them in case he's overcome with an urge to kill his father.'

77

My sarcasm bounced off him.

'Not at all. He's keeping them in case he becomes trapped in the mud in a shell crater with a troop of enemies advancing on him. Given what he's experienced it's a perfectly rational precaution, made inappropriate only by geographical location.'

'Meaning that he's not in the trenches any more?'

'Exactly. It will take him some time to become accustomed to that. Perhaps a lot of time. Meanwhile, he needs his weapons for reassurance.'

'I'm glad it's so simple.'

'Oh yes, he's easily my least interesting case. The degree of neurosis is surprisingly small now. It can best be treated by allowing him to remain in a peaceful place for a long time.'

'With a room full of weapons?'

'He has a very responsible attitude towards them. I'm quite satisfied that he's no danger to anybody.'

'You know he had two grenades stolen?'

If I'd hoped to surprise him, I'd failed again.

'Is that what he told you? Jack has these ideas from time to time. It's a not uncommon anxiety with hoarding behaviour.'

'You mean, they weren't stolen at all?'

'I don't know. I'm a psychologist, not a policeman. But I do know that Jack has a mild obsession about people stealing things from him.'

'Who else knows about these weapons?'

He smiled. 'Just about everybody, I should think.'

'That wasn't what Jack Kelso seemed to think. He asked me not to tell anybody.'

'That's part of a familiar pattern too. The subject wishes his hoard to remain secret but has a strong need that people should know of its existence. He resolved the contradiction by telling as many people as possible but swearing them to secrecy. You must have seen similar behaviour in children.'

'So he might have told anybody?'

'Indeed.'

'Don't you think you might have warned me?'

'There is such a thing as professional confidentiality, Miss Bray.'

'There is such a thing as professional overconfidence, Dr Stroud.'

David put in an appearance at dinner; also Stanley Gorton, who seemed subdued but ate as ferociously as usual. Over the fruit salad Jack Kelso caught my eye and gave me a long wink.

TEN

DREAMING'S NOT SOMETHING I OFTEN do, but there must have been something in the air at Nantgarrew. That night I dreamt I was holding a hand grenade with the pin taken out and I had to deliver it to somebody before it exploded, but I didn't know who. Then the lever of it came alive and was fighting in my hand like a snake. I woke sweating, seeing moonlight pouring in through the window where I'd left the curtains drawn back, knowing that something outside the dream had woken me. There'd been a noise somewhere, but I didn't know what kind of noise. I lay awake listening and thought I could hear somebody moving about downstairs. The moonlight was so bright that I didn't even have to strike a match to look at my watch. Just after two o'clock in the morning. I looked out of the window, over the silver glass of the conservatory and the dark rhododendron shrubbery to the bright streak of waterfall. No sign of anybody or anything.

It took me a few minutes to change into day clothes and go downstairs. I looked first into Dr Stroud's study and drew back the heavy curtains from the broken windows to let the light in, but the room was empty. So was Jenny's small office next door. When I went back to the hall I heard the noise again. It was coming from the kitchen regions at the back. I walked to the green baize door that shut off the staff corridor from the hall, making no effort to be quiet. The corridor itself was dark, but there was faint moonlight leaking from under the kitchen door and a scuffling sound behind it. I flung the door open.

A dark silhouette loomed in front of me by the kitchen

table. It was large and holding something in its hands.

'What are you doing? Put that down.'

The figure moved and something crashed down on the table. A man's voice spoke.

'It was left over. I didn't want it to go to waste.'

Stanley Gorton's voice, like a big child's.

I moved round so that the moonlight was on him and the thing on the table. It was a blue china bowl with the remains of the custard that had accompanied the fruit salad at dinner.

'It was only going to waste.'

He was staring piteously, first at me and then at the custard.

'I'm sorry to have interrupted you. I heard a noise downstairs and thought somebody might have broken in.'

He grinned with relief and picked up the bowl. As I closed the kitchen door I heard the glutinous slurp of a spoon coming out of cold custard.

I went upstairs slowly, intending to give the poor man time to finish his feast before I alerted Jenny. I thought she should know he was up and about because she'd seemed particularly concerned about Stanley and the place was, after all, a medical establishment. There was no answer to my gentle knock on her door. I tried again and, when there was still no answer, pushed open the door. The moonlight was streaming into her room as brightly as into mine onto a table, a chair and an empty bed with the bedclothes thrown back.

Something apart from Stanley Gorton must have woken Jenny in the middle of the night, otherwise she'd have gone straight to the kitchen and found him. She wasn't in the house downstairs or I'd have seen her. The only explanation was that she'd heard something and rushed outside, probably expecting to confront Mrs Minter, without having the sense to wake me. Alarmed, I hurried downstairs again and let myself out of the front door onto the lawn.

No sight or sound of anybody. When I looked back at the house all the windows were dark. Nothing was moving on the drive. I walked down the lawn towards the flagpole on the terrace. That was where the trouble had been last time, but now everything was quiet.

'Jenny?'

I called softly, experimentally. No answer. As I stood there wondering what to do next, I heard the shot.

It came from just below me and to my left, from the pasture on the far side of the bank. Just the one shot, then silence.

'Who's there?'

My voice echoed back from the other side of the valley. I thought I heard a scuffling from the other side of the bank, like somebody running away uphill.

'Jenny, are you there? I'm coming.'

My first thought was that Jenny had met Mrs Minter, tried to tackle her and the shot was the result. I ran up the bank, half fell, half scrambled down into the ditch on the other side of it. There was a barbed wire fence in front of me, the useless fence that Captain Hunter tended obsessively. The wire immediately in front of me was swaying. I couldn't see why until I looked along it and saw something hanging over the fence about ten yards away from me. Something too dark to be Jenny, and too heavy. Its falling had set the wire quivering all along the fence. The words of the song I'd heard the soldiers singing on the railway platform came into my mind and wouldn't go away.

'When you're hanging on the wire, Never Mind.
When you're hanging on the wire, Never Mind.
Though the light's as bright as day . . . '

I walked along the ditch until I was within a few feet of it. I could see what it was by then. A man in dark jacket and trousers, legs and buttocks towards me, bent looking over the fence, his toes on the strip of grass between the wire and the ditch. But he couldn't be looking over, not at that angle. I scrambled out of the ditch and up beside him, put my hand on his hip and had to stop myself screaming when he moved. Not a voluntary movement. He swung like a bundle of wet washing on a line, bent double over the top strand of barbed wire, weighing it down. Washing hung out to dry by moonlight.

'Though the light's as bright as day,
When you die they stop your pay.
When you're . . . '

I told myself not to be useless and hysterical. From the passivity of the swing I had no doubt that he was dead. The only question was his identity. I crawled under the wire to the rough pasture on the other side, knelt and raised the sagging head. The open eyes of Colonel Ralph Keyson stared into mine. The blankness of death had given his expression much the same touch of arrogance as in life. The curve of his aristocratic forehead was spoiled by a hole, a dense rim of tissue round it. When I felt his brain warm and slimy on my fingers I couldn't help letting the head drop, setting the whole bundle swinging again. There was a smaller wound on the back of his head, low down on the hairline to the left.

'The other one must be the exit wound.'

I heard my own voice saying it, sounding quite calm.

Colonel Keyson went on swinging on the wire, to and fro, gentle as the tide. Thousands of bodies must have swung like that over the past three years, in Flanders, on the Somme. Nothing special about Colonel Keyson at all. What was it Dr Stroud had said about Jack Kelso's box of grenades? Inappropriate only by geographical location. I heard my own voice saying that too. Then another voice from behind me, somebody coming down from the pasture to my right.

'Nell, what are you doing?'

David Ellward's voice.

What the war had done to David I only understood in the next few minutes. He came loping towards me, took the upper part of Keyson's body in his arms and gestured to me to get back to the other side and lift up the legs. We got it up and over the wire and David flopped it down onto the pasture as casually as if it had been a sack of potatoes. I remembered how, ten years and a lifetime ago, he'd been squeamish about picking up a bird that the cat had killed. He knelt beside Keyson, looking for a long time at the wound in the forehead. Then he lifted the head, let it loll forward and looked at the entry wound.

'I heard the shot.'

'Yes. He's still warm. As warm as a staff officer will ever be.'

He held up the wire and helped me crawl underneath it to his side, pulled a packet of cigarettes out of his pocket and offered one automatically to me.

'Sorry, Nell. I forgot you weren't my sergeant.'

He struck a match on the sole of his boot, lit a cigarette and sat on the grass smoking.

'Have to get a stretcher party organised, I suppose. No hurry, though.'

I made myself sit down too on the other side of Keyson's body, though further from it than he was.

I said, not looking at David: 'Did you kill him?'

'That's a good question. Did you?'

'David, please answer me.'

He glanced at me, then looked over the moonlit valley, dragging deeply on his cigarette.

'I'm a soldier, Nell. Soldiers are meant to kill people, aren't they?'

'You didn't.'

'If you say so.'

I looked to see what he was wearing. Shirt and trousers, no jacket.

'You're not carrying a gun.'

'No.'

'We must look for one, beside the body.'

He didn't seem interested. I walked to the point where I'd found the body and tried to guess how far a dying arm might throw a gun in the last reflex. Ten feet perhaps, twenty to make sure. There was no cover at all on the pasture side, just sheep-cropped grass with the wire fence

84

casting a moon shadow over it. I searched and found nothing, got down on my stomach to look beneath the fence, crawled under the wire to check the ditch and the bank on the other side. Nothing at all. All the while David smoked and watched me. I had another look under the fence then went back to sit beside him.

'It doesn't look as if he shot himself.'

'Oh, was that what you were doing? No, of course he didn't.'

'How did you know?'

'I thought you were observant. You were talking to yourself about exit wounds.'

'The one in his forehead.'

It seemed indecent to be discussing it with the body lying there between us, like making personal remarks about somebody.

'What side of his forehead?'

'Left of centre.'

'Yes. And what side's the entry wound at the back?'

'Left, low down.'

He knelt beside me and took my right arm. I tried to pull away from him.

'Relax Nell. I'm not going to shoot you. You're right-handed, so was he.'

He took my hand in his, drew it round to the back of my neck.

'Imagine there's a gun in your hand. You're going to shoot yourself. Do you do it like this?'

My arm was twisted awkwardly behind my neck, my knuckles on the point in the skull where the bullet had gone into Keyson.

'Is that how you'd do it?'

'No.'

He released my hand.

'Show me how, then.'

It was as much as I could do to keep my hand and voice steady.

'Like . . . Like this, I suppose, from the side.'

'Not in the back of your neck?'

'No. Or if I did, from the right side.'

'And if you decided, for some unknown reason, to do it from the left, I doubt if you could keep the gun straight enough to put a bullet neatly up and out of your left temple. It would have slanted. The exit wound would probably have been about here.'

Very lightly, he touched my forehead on the right, just below the hairline. His fingers were as cold as ice.

'Wouldn't you say so, Nell?'

He sat back on his heels and looked at me. The sharp profile, the long ridge of nose, were just as I remembered them, but he might have been a creature from another world.

I said: 'So he didn't kill himself. You must have heard the shot at least.'

'I'm always hearing shots.'

He fumbled in his pocket for the cigarette packet.

'I suppose one of us had better go to the house and tell them. You can go and I'll stay here with him, if you like. It won't be the first time.'

Go or stay, in this mood it wouldn't help. I took another look at him and the dark shape sprawled beside him, clambered into the ditch and up the bank and ran towards the house.

ELEVEN

ALL THE WINDOWS WERE DARK as I ran up the lawn towards the house. I remembered that I'd gone out to look for Jenny and still had no idea where she was. But as I was about to step off the grass and onto the gravel drive I saw a figure by the front door and thought it might be her. The figure was acting strangely, carrying something carefully and quietly down the steps. Whoever it was clearly hadn't heard me. I stayed where I was and kept quiet.

The figure wore some kind of soft cap and breeches. Its lower legs seemed thin, then I realised it was wearing puttees. It sat down on the front step and appeared to be doing something to its feet. Putting boots on. Whoever it was had crept out of the house on stockinged feet. As I watched it straightened up and hoisted the thing it had been carrying onto its back. Once he came out of the darkness of the porch I could see who it was. Even when trying to go quietly, Robin Duncan couldn't help walking like a young man in a raging temper. On his back was an army haversack. The mug and mess tin dangling from it gave an incongruous domestic touch. He walked on the grass at the side of the drive, obviously not wanting to make a noise on the gravel. When it was clear that he wasn't stopping to look back I followed him, as quietly as I could.

A little way down the drive he crossed it cautiously and disappeared into the shed where the bicycles were kept. I followed and waited outside the door, listening to clanking sounds from inside that suggested he was stumbling over things in the dark. He came out after a few minutes pushing a bicycle. I stepped forward.

'Where are you going?'

He couldn't help gasping and almost let go of the handlebars. He turned round.

'Are you spying on me?'

His eyes were hard and bright, his voice a hiss.

'I asked you where you're going.'

'Moscow. Are you going to try and stop me?'

'Moscow? On a bicycle?'

I think he believed I was laughing at him, and even in this situation he was young enough to resent that.

'On a ship, and I'm not letting you or anybody else here stop me.'

I stepped in front of him.

'I think you should wait. Do you know what's happened here tonight?'

'I don't bloody care what's happened here.'

'At least wait until the morning.'

He tried to push the bike round me. I dodged to the side and barred his way.

'I've warned you,' he said.

'You won't get far. At least tell me . . .'

'Will you get out of my way?'

His right hand went into the pocket of his jacket. When it came out I found myself, for the third time within twenty-four hours, looking down at a standard service revolver.

'Where did you get that?'

'It doesn't matter where I got it.'

He held it against my face, so close I could even smell the faint whiff of oil, the barrel cold on my cheekbone. His face was as hard as stone. I thought of the hole in Colonel Keyson's forehead. I stood aside. The moment I moved he was in the saddle and pedalling for all he was worth down the drive. He must have learned from Mrs Minter how fast a bicycle could go down that drive and I'd learned, from his lack of success in catching her, how futile it was to give chase on foot. I couldn't help running after him for a few paces, shouting to him to stop, but I knew it was a waste of effort. Ironic that I'd spent time and effort looking for the gun that killed Colonel Keyson. I'd probably just seen it at very close quarters.

I went into the house and upstairs, trying to work out which bedroom was Dr Stroud's. I settled for the first door on the left, knocked and heard his alarmed voice from inside.

'What's the matter? Who is it?'

'Nell Bray. Can you come out, please? Something's happened.'

He opened the door in pyjamas and dressing gown.

I said: 'Ralph Keyson's dead. Shot, out in the field on the fence. And Robin Duncan's run off.'

He looked at me, then disappeared back into his room without a word. He came out again almost immediately with brogues on his feet and an overcoat covering his pyjamas.

'Can you take me there?'

He followed me down the lawn without a word. It was getting light by then. As we clambered over the earth bank I said:

'David Ellward's with him. He arrived after I found him.'

He nodded but said nothing, helping me down into the ditch. As we were getting out on the far side I stopped.

'What's the trouble?'

'Two more people.'

I ran behind him along the strip of grass beside the fence. The body was lying as I'd last seen it, with David still sitting there beside it. Two more men were standing, looking down. Their backs were towards us but we could see the glow of their cigarettes cupped, soldier style, in backward facing palms. So that the enemy, out there in the Welsh dawn, should have no glowing spot to aim at. They heard us and turned.

'It's the doctor.'

Jack Kelso. The man standing next to him was Captain Hal Hunter.

Dr Stroud got to them a few strides before I did.

'What are you two doing here?'

Hal Hunter replied, making it sound like a report as usual.

'Sergeant Kelso and I were on our rounds when we heard a shot. We came over to investigate and saw Lieutenant Ellward keeping guard here beside the body.'

I said: 'It took you a long time to get here.'

Hal Hunter said nothing, but Jack seemed hurt.

'We didn't know where the shot came from at first, Miss. We wasted some time looking round.'

I stared at him and he stared back at me. It made no sense. Experienced soldiers like Captain Hunter and Sergeant Kelso would have known at once where the sound of one shot had come from on a quiet night. From the way Dr Stroud was looking at them, he was puzzled too. I asked Jack Kelso if they'd seen Robin Duncan.

'Not anybody, Miss, until we found Lieutenant Ellward here with the body.'

Dr Stroud said abruptly: 'I'd better have a look at him.'

'He's as dead as they come, Sir.'

Dr Stroud knelt down, looked at the gaping wound in the forehead then, as David had done, turned the body over. He laid it gently down again and looked at me.

'Where was he when you found him?'

I led him to the place on the wire. In the grey light you could see the pool of blood and brains where the head had hung. Captain Hunter and Jack Kelso followed us but David stayed where he was, by the body.

Jack Kelso said: 'Funny he should do it on the wire.'

Stroud gave him a sharp look.

'Are you saying he shot himself?'

'What else, Sir, unless the madwoman did it? And I don't think even she's mad enough for that.'

I said: 'If he shot himself, where's the gun?'

Very soon, Dr Stroud would have to know about the gun in Robin Duncan's hands, but I didn't want to come out with it before the rest of them. A man on a bicycle couldn't get far away and I was reluctant to be the one to put the young man before a firing squad, even if he had killed

90

Colonel Keyson.

They looked down at their feet. Jack Kelso said:

'If his arm jerked it might have gone a bit of a distance.'

'That's what I thought,' I said. 'I looked. I couldn't find it.'

Captain Hunter said sharply: 'It must be here somewhere.'

He obviously didn't rate my powers of observation highly. He started organising everybody.

'You hop over the wire, sergeant, and take the top sector. I'll take the lower one. Ellward, you take the top sector on the other side, especially the ditch.'

Dr Stroud had knelt by the pool of blood and brains. He looked up.

'I'll do the lower section if you like, Hal.'

His voice was calm and I thought he was humouring Hunter. He scrambled up and looked down ruefully at his overcoat. There was a patch of something dark and sticky where he'd been kneeling. When he pulled a hank of grass and started rubbing at it, even the soldiers looked away.

Hal Hunter said sharply: 'We'd better get on with it.'

As I'd been given no orders and was sure it was a waste of time anyway, I watched while the others searched. David and Dr Stroud went about it mechanically, Hunter and Jack Kelso with more enthusiasm.

'Nothing here, Sir.'

'Very well, sergeant. Take two paces out and try again.'

It was full daylight, and David and Dr Stroud had already given up, before the two of them came back to the fence. Jack Kelso was beginning to tell us they'd found nothing when Captain Hunter stopped suddenly, in the act of climbing back over the fence.

'There it is.'

He pointed at the foot of a fence post, two feet or so up the hill from the puddle of brains and blood.

'It was there all the time, right by the fence.'

Dr Stroud said quickly: 'Leave it there.'

All of us except David crowded round it. A service revolver, looking exactly like the one that Jacko had

91

offered to me or the two that Monica Minter and Robin Duncan had pointed at me, was lying by the post, butt towards us. Disregarding Dr Stroud, Captain Hunter picked it up, sniffed at the barrel and looked inside it.

'Yes, it's been fired. I knew it must be here somewhere.'

He held it by the barrel and offered it to Dr Stroud, who took it awkwardly, glanced at it and handed it back.

'I don't think we should be touching it, Hal. We should have left it where it was, for the police to see.'

'With respect, Sir, I don't think that will matter much. It's clear enough what happened. He stands right up by the wire, shoots himself in the back of the head, arm jerks out and catches on the wire probably so the gun lands there, more or less where you'd expect.'

I waited for David to explain, as he'd explained to me, how Keyson couldn't have shot himself in that way. He said nothing. He wasn't even looking at us.

I said: 'It wasn't there when I looked about forty minutes ago.'

All of them except David turned to look at me.

'If that gun had been there then, I'd have found it.'

Hal Hunter said patronisingly: 'Your nerves would naturally have been shaken, Miss Bray.'

'Not so shaken that my brain wasn't working. The first place I thought of looking was by the fence posts.'

Jack Kelso said, trying to be kind: 'It wasn't light then, Miss. Anyway, you wouldn't have wanted to go treading in the blood and so on. Anybody could have missed it.'

'David, you were there when I was looking. You must have seen me checking round the posts.'

He dragged his attention back to me from a long way off. I had to repeat what I'd said, and even then he took his time about answering.

'I'm sorry, Nell. I didn't really notice where you were looking. It must have been there all the time after all.'

I stared at him, trying to let him know what I thought of this betrayal. It was all too clearly a conspiracy among the three of them. Whether David thought he was covering up for Hal Hunter and Jack Kelso, or they were covering up for him or all three of them for Robin Duncan, I was up against a soldiers' pact, forged by forces I'd never known. Dr Stroud was looking from one to the other of us. I think he'd guessed what was going on and was trying to decide what to do about it.

'We must report it. I'm going back to the house to send the boy to Abergavenny for the police. Jack, if you'll come back with me we can fetch a stretcher. Hal, you'd better keep that gun for the moment, but mark the place where you found it. The police will want to know. And you'd better not handle it any more than you can help. They might want to check it for his fingerprints.'

I caught up with him half way across the lawn.

'I suppose you'll have to tell the police about Robin Duncan too. He threatened me with a revolver not long after this happened. He took a bicycle and said he was going to Moscow.'

Dr Stroud gave a quick nod and went striding on. Jack Kelso came jogging after us, still concerned for my tender feelings.

'You mustn't worry about not seeing that gun, Miss Bray. You've kept a hold of yourself very well, considering.'

It was no use saying anything.

When we got to the house Dr Stroud and Jack Kelso disappeared into the back regions in search of the gardening boy and a stretcher. It was still half dark in the hall and I noticed a line of lamplight coming from under the closed door of Dr Stroud's study. I pushed it open and went in. Jenny was standing by the desk, next to a big filing cabinet. She was fully dressed but her hair was all over the place and her eyes had a wild look. The top drawer of the cabinet was open and files and sheets of paper were strewn over the desk. She jumped when I came in and dropped a file.

'Nell, what's happening?'

I put my arm round her and made her sit down in a chair that had survived the grenade explosion.

'I'm sorry, Jenny. I'm afraid Colonel Keyson is dead. I found him outside near the fence, early this morning.'

Her mouth gaped open. She slumped against me, then

pulled herself away as if any touch hurt her.

'How?'

It was more a groan than a question.

'He'd been shot in the head.'

She slumped down over the desk. I knelt on the floor beside her.

'Jenny, I'm sorry.'

She was shaking convulsively, trying to say something, but she'd wrapped her arms round her head and I couldn't hear what it was.

'Don't try to talk, Jenny. Not yet.'

She lay there for several minutes, her back heaving with great, dry sobs. Then she struggled to pull herself upright and twisted round to look at me.

'It was that woman. That wicked, wicked woman.'

My heart sank.

'Jenny, I really don't think this has anything to do with Mrs Minter.'

I didn't intend, certainly not at this point, to say anything about Robin Duncan or the conspiracy of the other three.

'But it was. I saw her. She must have been getting away after she'd done it. I wish I'd known. I wish . . . oh . . .'

Her words died away into a wail. Her fingers were rubbing hard up and down her face, almost clawing it.

'Jenny, my poor Jenny, where did you think you'd seen her?'

I thought it was hysteria, that Jenny in her shock and grief was seizing on the person she liked least to blame for it. She sensed that and pounded on my shoulder with her fist.

'Nell, I'm not mad. Listen to me. I was in bed. I heard a noise, somebody going downstairs. I got up and dressed.'

'What time was this?'

'Ten past one.'

'You're sure of that?'

'Yes. Listen. While I was getting dressed I heard somebody unlocking the front door and going out. I thought it was one of the patients and I'd better see what

94

was happening. By the time I got outside there was no sign of anybody, so I walked down the drive. I'd lit a lamp and taken it with me, only it was moonlight anyway. I got to the bottom of the drive, then I saw her.'

'Where?'

She was telling it calmly now, but I sensed the hysteria underneath.

'Walking along the road. I ran after her and shouted, "Where are you going?" I was quite close to her when she turned round. I saw her as clearly as I'm seeing you.'

'What did she do?'

'She . . . she sort of sneered at me. A really evil look. She had a bicycle leaning against the gate post. She just jumped on it and went off. I was so furious, I ran after her.'

'You must have known you couldn't catch her.'

'Yes, but I was so angry I had to do something. I felt I could run all the way down to where she lives if I had to.'

'But you didn't?'

My fear that she was hysterical was giving place to a worse worry. Half an hour or so after this would have happened, soon after two o'clock, I'd been up and about myself. I'd looked for Jenny but hadn't found her.

'No. I'd run quite a long way, at least, it felt like a long way, then I twisted my ankle. I thought I'd hurt it badly. I just sat there on a pile of stones, then I thought I couldn't stay there all night so I managed to get myself back. I came in here and found somebody had broken the lock on Dr Stroud's cabinet.'

'Is anything missing?'

'That was what I was trying to find out when you came in. I'm nearly sure some of the patients' records have gone.'

'Anything else?'

'Yes, his latest notes for the book. Everything's all out of order. I was trying to check what had been taken when you came in and . . .'

She started crying. In telling her story about Mrs Minter I think she'd distracted herself for a while from the worse thing that followed.

'I thought then . . . that was what she'd been doing . . .

95

breaking in to take the records and notes. If I'd known what she'd done as well I'd have caught up with her if I'd had to do it on my knees.'

I stroked her hair and shoulders, trying to calm her, but my mind was only half with her. I was by no means convinced that she really had seen Monica Minter. But if she had that made things even more complicated. Hal Hunter and the others would never try to cover up a murder by Mrs Minter. As for the raid on the files, that seemed such a minor thing in the face of murder that it made no sense. Had Robin Duncan wanted to take his medical records to Moscow? Had Stanley Gorton broken in and eaten them?

I heard noises from out at the back that I thought were probably Dr Stroud and Jack Kelso going out with a stretcher. I didn't want Jenny to think about that.

'I'm going to take you up to bed, then I'll get you some warm milk.'

'I couldn't sleep. Julius will need me.'

'He can wait for an hour or two.'

I helped her up. I wanted to look at her ankle but she wouldn't let me. She moved stiffly, limping a little, and I noticed that her skirt was dusty and her shoes badly scuffed and scratched. These things, at any rate, supported part of her story. I hated to have to think about Jenny in that way, but what it had come to was that I didn't believe anybody at Nantgarrew.

I persuaded her to lie down on her bed then went down to the kitchen to heat some milk, noticing that Stanley Gorton had rinsed and put away the custard bowl. When I took the milk to her Jenny was sitting up in bed with a blanket round her legs.

'Jenny, I'm sorry to ask this, but did you hear a shot at any time?'

She nodded. 'When I was running after her down the road.'

'In that case, how could she have shot him?'

'I don't know. If she didn't, who did? Oh God.'

Tears ran down her face. I went to the chest of drawers

to fetch a handkerchief for her and tripped over something that had been propped against a chair. It turned out to be the photograph of Dr Freud that Jenny must have carried upstairs with her for safe keeping. A piece of picture wire or somesuch got itself caught round the heel of my shoe and had to be untangled. When Jenny saw what I was doing her sobs came harder. The picture must have reminded her, as it reminded me, of the grenade attack and what had seemed, at the time, a lucky escape from death. I found Jenny the handkerchief then carried the picture away with me to my room so that it shouldn't distress her any more. I turned its face to the wall and went downstairs in time to see Jack Kelso and Hal Hunter carrying a blanket-covered form on a stretcher into a room off the hall.

TWELVE

I WENT OUTSIDE FOR AIR. It was still early, not yet six o'clock, on the morning of a June day that looked likely to be as fine as the ones before it. The sky was cloudless. A blackbird was hopefully looking for worms on the dried-up lawn. As I watched, it found what looked like a fine long one, then twitched its head and threw it away. Curious to see what would make a bird discard such a meal, I went closer. The bird flew away in a flurry of warning notes and I found myself looking down not at a worm but at a long piece of red rubber.

It must have been about eighteen inches long and more than an inch wide. It was new, very flexible, with a dusting of French chalk still on one side of it. A piece of a cycle tyre inner tube, not torn as it might be after a puncture but very carefully cut. I remembered, for some reason, what Jenny had said about ordering a new inner tube from Abergavenny, and the tube's disappearance. Vandalism of a petty kind. My mind was only running on it at all as a distraction from the things it should be dealing with. Still, if only to save another blackbird from disappointment, I rolled up the piece of rubber and put it in my pocket.

Some time afterwards Dr Stroud came out to join me as I was walking up and down on the lawn.

'Ten steps one way, then ten steps the other, Miss Bray. Do I detect a minor compulsion neurosis?'

'Oh dear, am I still doing that? It was the size of a cell in Holloway prison quite a long time ago.'

It was, I knew, a habit that returned only when I was

very worried. He probably guessed that, but made no comment. We covered two widths of the lawn in silence before he spoke.

'We need to talk, don't we, Miss Bray?'

'Have you sent for the police?'

'Yes. I sent the boy off on Miss Chesney's bicycle. My own seems to have disappeared.'

'I think that was the one Robin Duncan took.'

'Ah yes. Robin.'

We turned at the edge of the lawn and began walking back.

'Did you tell the police about him too?'

'I thought it best to keep things simple for the moment. I simply said in my note that there'd been an accident and a man was dead. It will probably be another hour before they get here. That gives us a little time.'

Another silence. I was beginning to realise that Dr Stroud expected me to read a lot from his silences. I, on the other hand, was determined that he should put things into words.

'A little time for what?'

'To decide what we're going to tell them.'

'About Robin?'

'Among other things.'

'Very well, let's start with Robin. I hear a shot. I find Colonel Keyson shot through the head. About forty minutes later I see Robin Duncan trying to leave secretly. When I try to stop him he threatens me with a revolver.'

'And that leads you to what conclusion?'

'I'm not drawing any conclusions. I'm stating facts.'

I was trying to re-live the moment when Robin held the revolver against my cheek. I remembered the faint smell of oil. If he'd shot Colonel Keyson with the gun, wouldn't it have smelled strongly of cordite? A soldier could tell me, but there wasn't a soldier there I could trust.

'Would Robin Duncan wish to kill Colonel Keyson?'

'You know him better than I do. What do you think?'

He shrugged. 'It would depend on the circumstances.'

'So do most things. Suppose Robin had made an earlier

99

attempt to escape last night and Colonel Keyson had tried to stop him.'

'It sounds as if you've decided that Robin killed him.'

'No. If he did, that leaves us with another problem. He could hardly have come back without anybody seeing him and put that revolver by the fence post.'

Silence. I took it to imply scepticism.

'Dr Stroud, I didn't argue with Hal Hunter and Jack Kelso about this because there was no point. But I'm as sure as I've ever been sure of anything that the gun was not there when I looked for it just after I found him. In fact, that's almost the only thing I am sure of.'

We turned round and were half way across the lawn before he spoke again.

'Accepting what you say, what conclusion do we draw from that?'

'As far as I can see, one of three people must have put it there: David Ellward, Jack Kelso, Hal Hunter. Or perhaps all three of them together.'

'Why would they do that?'

'You know as well as I do.'

Another few paces. I noticed that the lawn was drying in irregular patches of brown grass, like a creature with the mange.

'To protect somebody?'

'Yes. To protect whoever killed him by making it look like suicide.'

'Where would they get a revolver?'

'Jack Kelso had two of them yesterday. Even if Robin Duncan stole one, that still leaves another.'

The clatter of somebody putting out breakfast things was coming from inside the house. I wondered if Megan and the cook knew yet that Keyson was dead. Probably not.

'Of course, they all disliked poor Ralph.'

'That's putting it mildly.'

I thought of the way David had handled the body. So far Dr Stroud had said nothing to remind me that he knew of my special interest in him. I was grateful for that at least.

I said: 'I have no doubt at all that any one of those three would try to protect the others. The question is, would they do the same for Robin? I had the impression that they didn't like him very much.'

'No. A lonely young man in many ways.'

'In any case, if they were protecting Robin with that gun trick, they'd have had to know in the first place that Robin killed him. I don't see when he'd have had the time to tell them.'

'Unless it was a plot among the four of them and young Robin was chosen to pull the trigger.'

At last a positive contribution from Dr Stroud. I was sorry to criticise it.

'In that case, wouldn't they have made some more efficient arrangement for his escape? The least they could have done was have his pack and the bicycle out ready for him.'

'Yes, I suppose so.'

A figure had come out onto the porch. It was Stanley Gorton, field glasses to his eyes, looking out over the valley. When we looked in the same direction we saw two great birds soaring.

'Did you know Stanley Gorton was up and about in the early hours? That was what woke me. I found him in the kitchen eating custard.'

'He often does that.'

We stood still and watched the circling birds.

'Then there's Jenny. She's quite convinced she saw Mrs Minter at the bottom of the drive at some time after one o'clock last night.'

He jumped.

'What was she doing out at that time?'

'She says she heard somebody going out soon after one. It might have been Colonel Keyson himself, I suppose. Anyway, she went down the drive to the road and is convinced she saw Mrs Minter with a sneering expression on her face. She chased after her until she hurt her ankle.'

This account seemed to disturb him as much as anything.

'When did she tell you this?'

'When I found her in your study.' It occurred to me that Jenny would have had no chance to tell him about the papers. 'I'm afraid she seemed to think that somebody had broken into your filing cabinet.'

'Oh God, what's gone?'

'Some notes and records, she thinks. She was trying to find out when I came in and had to tell her about Ralph Keyson. It was a bad blow to her. I have the impression that she was very fond of him.'

I looked at his face. It was important to me to know just how fond of Ralph Keyson Jenny had been and whether it was common knowledge at Nantgarrew.

'Yes.'

His tone and expression gave nothing away.

'I had to put her to bed. She said you'd need her, but she was in no condition to do anything.'

'Of course not.'

He sounded abstracted. The possible reappearance of Mrs Minter and the raid on his files was clearly another bad blow.

'Miss Bray, you've known Jenny for some time. Do you think she really saw Mrs Minter?'

'I don't know.'

I said it reluctantly.

'If she did, what would that signify?'

'As far as Colonel Keyson's death is concerned, it wouldn't necessarily signify anything. She might have been here simply to get her hands on your records.'

He looked sick at the thought of his patients' records in her possession.

'That bloody woman.'

'I suppose we have to tell the police about her too.'

He turned and looked me in the face.

'Yes, that's the question we've been discussing, isn't it? What exactly we tell the police and, more to the point, my military superior Brigadier Moss.'

'I was under the impression we were discussing who killed Colonel Keyson.'

'Have you considered the consequences of a murder inquiry at Nantgarrew? Brigadier Moss would be only too pleased to close us down and declare all the men here fit to return to combat. This would be the excuse he needs.'

He didn't have to say David's name to make me aware of the moral arm-twisting.

'I should have thought even the suicide of a colonel would be excuse enough.'

'Soldiers do kill themselves sometimes, even Brigadier Moss must accept that. And Ralph Keyson was a very troubled man.'

It was my turn to be silent.

'After all, Miss Bray, the only compelling argument against suicide is your belief that the gun was put there at some time after death.'

'My certainty. And there's something else. I don't see how he could have put a bullet through his own head at that angle.'

'Any person is in an unusual state of mind when he takes his own life.'

'Does that include contortionism?'

He winced.

We walked across the lawn and back, across and back. Stanley Gorton went back inside. Dr Caspian, the padre and another of his patients watched us from the terrace by the French windows. They kept their distance, as if disaster might be catching. By now the police from Abergavenny must be well on their way up the valley, followed by the military authorities all the way from Newport. They were all of them at Nantgarrew subject to military discipline, and killing an officer would mean the firing squad. Robin Duncan had already made himself a deserter the moment his stolen bicycle wheels passed the end of the drive. Add that to incitement to mutiny and his future looked bleak when the authorities caught up with him, even without a murder charge.

I said: 'You're asking me to keep quiet about anything that points away from suicide?'

'I can't ask you to do anything. I can only talk about the

consequences.'

Nantgarrew closed. And whatever the oddity of Dr Freud's theories, they might at least keep a few men out of the war. One of those men quite probably a murderer. Twenty thousand dead on the first day of the Somme. How much did one murder matter any more?

I said: 'You'll have to make sure that the other three have worked out their stories.'

'Yes.'

If he knew he'd won a victory he was too intelligent to let it show.

'And even if you don't tell them about Robin Duncan now, they'll realise he's missing sooner or later.'

'Yes.'

We were heading back to the house now, to coffee and breakfast.

'Just one more thing, Dr Stroud.'

He was in a hurry now, things settled, wanting to get to his records and see the damage.

'What's that?'

'I'll co-operate in lying to the police and the military authorities because I don't want to be responsible for the death of any of these men. But I want to know who killed Ralph Keyson and I'm going to do all I can to find out.'

He looked at me and nodded. At least I didn't have to argue with him, as I'd argued with Robin, that one life mattered. Even if it was a staff officer's life.

Before going in for breakfast I looked in on Jenny. As I'd hoped, she was deeply asleep and hardly stirred when I opened the door and tiptoed in. She was lying on her side. One hand, still clutching a rolled-up handkerchief, was pressed to her cheek and an ankle was sticking out from the blanket. I went softly to cover it up. It must have been the injured one because it was wound round with a bandage. A very odd bandage, khaki-coloured and tied round with string, one end of it cut off jaggedly, as if with a knife. I drew the blanket over it and went out without waking her, taking one more puzzle down to breakfast with me. Why should Jenny, who claimed to have injured her ankle chasing Mrs Minter down the road, have bandaged it with, of all things, part of a soldier's puttee?

THIRTEEN

THE POLICE ARRIVED BEFORE BREAKFAST was over, an inspector and a constable who'd driven up the valley from Abergavenny. They were respectful, which might have had something to do with the fact that Dr Stroud assumed his military rank for once. The combination of a dead colonel and a live major was enough to make them tread with some care. But for all that the inspector was thorough. He asked me to lead them to the place where I'd found Keyson and to go over my story of hearing the shot. By agreement with Dr Stroud, I'd edited it a little to leave out Stanley Gorton in the kitchen. I said simply that I thought I'd heard somebody going downstairs, so had followed. I said nothing about going to look for Jenny. If I'd mentioned that the police would have wanted to question her as well, which would have brought in the whole business of Mrs Minter. What we wanted was a nice uncomplicated suicide and, at first, it looked as if that was what we were getting.

David, Jack Kelso and Hal Hunter went one by one to give their evidence, into Jenny's typing room that had been commandeered by the police. I knew what they'd be saying because it was exactly what we'd agreed in a hasty discussion over the breakfast coffee. They'd been unable to sleep and had decided to go for a walk by moonlight. They too had heard the shot and come to find me by the body. The deceased's weapon was found by Captain Hunter soon afterwards. If the police showed signs of being suspicious of the mass outbreak of insomnia at Nantgarrew, as well they might, it would be Dr Stroud's job to remind the police that these were all men suffering from war neurosis. I'd no doubt that he'd do it very well, stressing the mentally wounded warriors aspect and leaving out the more extreme theories of Dr Freud. It would take a callous policeman, after all, to cast doubts on the likes of Sergeant Jack Kelso, Military Medal.

It was also Dr Stroud's task to provide for the police evidence that Colonel Keyson had been in a state of mind in which he might take his own life. I wished I could have eavesdropped on that. Jenny had told me about the nightmares that had sent the Colonel to Nantgarrew but in the short time I'd known him I'd seen no signs of abnormality. But again, the idea of a senior officer driven to suicide by the loss of his men was something that a decent patriotic policeman might find hard to question. Or so we hoped. It alarmed me to find how much, in the past few hours, I'd identified myself with the rest of Nantgarrew in trying to deceive the authorities.

They left in the afternoon. The inspector took the revolver away with him, wrapped carefully in a cloth. When he'd heard that Captain Hunter and Dr Stroud had handled it he'd got them to press their fingers onto glass slides, for comparison. Before the police left a covered van had arrived for the body. My sense of relief as I watched the two vehicles driving away down the valley road was mingled with unease that the two things which could disprove our story – the body with the bullet's path and the gun itself – had gone out of our control. I turned to see Dr Stroud behind me. He gave a quick twist of a smile.

'Now we have to worry about Brigadier Moss.'

As he left, Jenny limped up to me.

'What did he say?'

It surprised me that she had to ask for information about Dr Stroud from me. It was a reminder that Jenny was outside our inner circle of conspiracy. There was, too, a division between us that we both sensed. I didn't believe her story of what she'd been doing the night before, and she guessed that. I asked her if she'd managed to discover what records had been stolen from the filing cabinet, then bit my tongue when I remembered that she'd had no chance because Colonel Keyson's body had only just been taken away from the study.

'Dr Stroud looked. Some of the most recent files have gone, with notes I hadn't typed up yet. But the worst of it is, a whole chapter from his book. He didn't keep a copy.'

There was the noise of a motor vehicle climbing the drive. Jenny, already pale, turned paler.

'It's Brigadier Moss. Oh, Nell.'

She bolted into the house, presumably to warn Dr Stroud.

I'd expected somebody formidable and at first glance was disappointed. The driver jumped down to open the door for him, saluting smartly, and Brigadier Moss took his time in climbing down. He was in his late fifties, dressed for the riding school rather than a motor car journey in tunic, breeches and highly polished boots with spurs. He was thin to the point of being skeletal and the face above the highly pressed uniform had a yellowish tinge, with the look of a lecturer in classics at some minor university. There was an air of disappointment about him, but a very superior kind of disappointment, as if the world consistently failed to come up to his standards.

Dr Stroud, looking nervous but still defiantly in civilian dress, met him on the steps. Then they were closeted together in Jenny's office for nearly an hour. While this was going on the rest of us stayed near the house, on the lawn or the path leading to the waterfall. Treatment for Dr Stroud's patients had been suspended for the day, but Dr Caspian was struggling to maintain some kind of routine, mostly consisting of organised games. As for the four of us in what I thought of as the inner ring of conspiracy, we seemed to make a point of avoiding each other. Jack Kelso, making himself useful as usual, had fetched hammer and nails and was repairing a rose trellis that had pulled away from the wall. Captain Hunter was sitting on the garden seat near the flagpole, reading a book on Hannibal. From where he was sitting he could see all the way down the drive, so perhaps he still thought of

108

himself as being on guard duty. David was clearly restive because Dr Stroud had asked him, as a favour, not to disappear on one of his long walks. The last time I'd seen him he was sitting on the rocks by the waterfall, casting an occasional stone into the pool.

One by one we were called in to see the Brigadier, first Hal Hunter, then David, then Jack Kelso. Jack was in there for more than half an hour. Afterwards he came across the lawn to find me, looking red and flurried.

'Do you know where Miss Chesney is?'

'No. What's up? Does Brigadier Moss want her?'

He shook his head.

'No. It's you he wants to see next, Miss. Only there's something I wanted to tell Miss Chesney. It doesn't matter.'

But from his face it clearly did. It struck me like a blow that Brigadier Moss had been asking him about Jenny's relationship with Colonel Keyson.

'We'll go and find Jenny together. Brigadier Moss will have to wait.'

That clearly alarmed him.

'Oh no, Miss, better not keep him waiting. It's all right.'

But his usual cheerfulness was now quite gone.

I knocked on the door of Jenny's office and walked in. Brigadier Moss was standing behind the desk. He made no move to shake hands and neither did I.

'Would you sit down please, Miss Bray.'

It was like going to the dentist. I sat down and he took his place behind Jenny's desk. The typewriter had been removed and all he had in front of him was an official notebook. He took the top off his fountain pen as slowly as peeling off a glove.

'Well, Miss Bray.'

He stared at me as if I'd presented him with an inadequate piece of Greek prose. If this was supposed to intimidate me, the man was a fool after all. As I said nothing, he was forced into longer speech.

'It's a surprise to find you here. I understand you have a heavy programme of speaking engagements.'

'Yes indeed. The number of anti-war rallies is increasing all the time.'

He pretended to consult his notebook.

'I see your next public appearance is in Manchester.'

'Yes. I'm glad the posters are up already.'

But it was a surprise that he knew about it. His interests must be wider than I'd realised.

'Do you spend much time at Nantgarrew?'

He managed, by the way he pronounced the name, to make it sound disreputable.

'This is my first visit. I arrived less than forty-eight hours ago to visit a friend who works here.'

'And in spite of having been here for less than forty-eight hours, you decided to go out for a walk in the early hours of this morning?'

'I don't see what the length of time has to do with it. I thought I heard somebody downstairs, so I got up to look.'

He raised his eyebrows. They were very dark and so precise in shape that they might have been put on with greasepaint.

'Indeed. Wouldn't it have been advisable to wake one of the doctors, or your friend Miss Chesney?'

Damn the man. He seemed to have an instinct for the weak point.

'I didn't want to wake up hard-working people unless it was necessary.'

'And you decided that it wasn't necessary?'

'No. Not at that point.'

He leaned forward, elbows on the desk, keeping his eyes on my face.

'And that was in spite of the fact that two people had been almost killed in a grenade attack the day before.'

I wished Dr Stroud had warned me but knew he could hardly have helped telling Brigadier Moss about that. One look into the room next door would have been enough.

Brigadier Moss leaned back, smiling a thin, precise smile.

'Well, Miss Bray?'

'Nobody was throwing grenades last night.'

110

'No, Miss Bray. Somebody was shooting last night, just as somebody was shooting six days ago.'

'Six days ago? I wasn't . . .'

'I know you weren't here then, but I'm sure you'll have heard about it since. Were you or were you not aware that a shot had been fired last Sunday at three officers in the conservatory?'

'I was aware, yes.'

'And yet last night, hearing, as you say, somebody downstairs, you got up without making any attempt to rouse anybody else and went down to see what was happening. I find that a little hard to believe.'.

I said nothing, telling myself that I must only respond to direct questions. I was in a quicksand and would make things worse by threshing around.

After a long silence, during which I tried to catch him blinking and didn't, he made a note in his book and sighed.

'Leaving that question aside for a moment, let's move on to your discovery of Colonel Keyson's body.'

As I'd done for the police, I went through the process of hearing the shot and finding the body.

'So did you at last go for assistance, Miss Bray?'

'As you'll have been told already, I didn't need to. Lieutenant Ellward was on the scene almost immediately, Captain Hunter and Sergeant Kelso soon afterwards.'

'How convenient.'

I didn't rise to that sneer. I wondered if he'd learned somehow about my old friendship with David Ellward and told myself it was unlikely.

I should never have let the thought into my mind. Somehow he must have picked it up.

'You've told me that you've been here for almost forty-eight hours. Did you, during that time, witness any hostility between Colonel Keyson and any of the other patients here?'

'No.'

It was hardly a lie. I hadn't witnessed the argument between Keyson and David. The one between Keyson and Stanley Gorton was too petty to be called hostility.

'You weren't present, then, at the argument between Colonel Keyson and Captain Ellward?'

I was so angry that I felt like rushing out of the room and shaking somebody. But there were the cold eyes and the poised pen to deal with.

'You tell me there was an argument. If there was, I was not present at it.'

He made another note. Part of his technique, nothing to be nervous about. I could feel my calves twitching, not from nervousness but from a desire to be out of that room doing something, anything.

'We've established, Miss Bray, that you knew about the shot fired into the conservatory. Have you had any conversation with anybody about that?'

'It was mentioned by various people.'

'Do you think Colonel Keyson might have been the intended target on that occasion?'

'How could I possibly know that? But from what I've been told, he was the furthest away. Lieutenant Gorton seems to have been most at risk.'

He made another note. Surely I'd told him nothing he hadn't discovered already.

'And the grenade attack yesterday, I gather you witnessed that.'

'No, I did not witness it. I heard the explosion and came running up afterwards.'

'Were you aware that nobody here had seen fit to inform the authorities about these two incidents?'

'That's hardly my business.'

We stared at each other, then he sighed again and told me he had no more questions.

'For the moment, that is. For the moment.'

I found Dr Stroud talking to Jenny in the porch. Both of them looked worried, Jenny near to tears, but I was too angry to worry about that.

'Did you tell Brigadier Moss about the conservatory?'

'No.'

'Well, one of the others must have done. Where's Captain Hunter?'

'It wasn't him either. It wasn't any of us. He already knew.'

'How?'

'I don't know.'

'You might have warned me.'

'I'm sorry. There seems so much to think about. I'm very sorry.'

No good raging at him. It was obviously as much as he could do to hold his own nerve together. While we were standing there, Brigadier Moss's driver came out of the house. He came to attention in front of Dr Stroud.

'Message from Brigadier Moss, Sir. He wishes to speak to another of your patients.'

'Which one?'

'Corporal Robin Duncan.'

The driver's tone was respectful, but you could sense dislike behind it. He turned on his heel and marched back into the house. Jenny's hands went to her face.

'Oh God, what do we do now?'

FOURTEEN

Brigadier Moss practically spat the word at Dr Stroud, standing in the porch, booted legs apart. Jenny had tactfully disappeared before he came out to see what was causing the delay. I stayed.

'You are aware that this is a case of desertion?'

'Yes, I'm aware of that.'

Dr Stroud's voice was weary.

'Say "Sir" when you address me.'

Brigadier Moss's voice was like a blow.

'Yes, Sir, I am aware it is a case of desertion. But I would point out that this is a hospital for . . . '

'It's still a military establishment. What do you propose to do about it?'

'Clearly, we'll have to look for him . . . Sir.'

'And how do you propose to set about that? When was this man last seen? Was he present at morning roll call?'

'You'll appreciate, Sir, that things were confused this morning.'

'Meaning you didn't take a roll call? What about last night?'

I already knew enough about Nantgarrew to be sure that roll calls formed no part of its routine. Dr Stroud did his best.

'He was present at the evening meal.'

'So for all we know he may have disappeared during the night?'

'Yes Sir.'

'For heaven's sake, man, he could be thirty miles away by now.'

At least he didn't know about the bicycle and I certainly wouldn't be the one to tell him. The Brigadier's reaction to Robin's disappearance had at least confirmed one thing for me. Whether he'd shot Keyson or not, I was in no hurry to hand him back to the system that made a death sentence out of a word.

I watched, through the late afternoon and evening, as search parties were organised. David, along with two of Dr Caspian's more athletic patients, was detailed to search the hill ridges. He set off, swinging an ash stick and looking more like a hiker than a soldier, and I knew that he at least would be out of the way for hours. Sergeant Kelso, the driver and the Padre were sent marching up the valley road, the Padre roaring out 'Onward Christian Soldiers' as they went, in a surprisingly strong baritone. Brigadier Moss drove himself down the valley, Dr Stroud sitting uncomfortably beside him, to interrogate the local farmers. The sun was down on the top of the hills by the time they got back and Brigadier Moss's temper had not improved. When he found that none of his other search parties had any success he announced he was going back to Newport to begin a wider hunt.

'At the moment, I've no alternative but to leave you in charge here, Major Stroud. You may expect to hear from me.'

That was said in front of Dr Caspian and several patients as Brigadier Moss climbed into his motor car. Dr Stroud made no reply and the car roared away down the drive, the staccato bursts of its engine seeming to make their own military comment on the state of affairs at Nantgarrew.

Jenny came out when the car drove away, face full of questions, hands clasped together so hard they must have been hurting each other.

'He'll find him, won't he?'

'Yes, I'm afraid so. Unless we find him first.'

They all looked at me. The idea had only just come into my head.

'What do you mean, Nell?'

'We have two advantages. We know about the bicycle and we know where he's making for.'

'But if you find him?'

I looked at Dr Stroud.

'I don't think you should know any more about this . . . Major Stroud.'

He was in enough trouble. In any case, I didn't know myself what I'd do when and if I found Robin, beyond asking him a few important questions. It was for the sake of those questions, at least as much as for his own skin, that I wanted to find him before Brigadier Moss did.

I made myself take three hours' sleep. I'd had little enough the night before and there was a long walk ahead of me. It turned out that Jenny's bicycle had been abandoned by the gardening boy at a repair shop in Abergavenny, when the slow puncture became a fast one during his rush for the police. Although I refused to answer any of Jenny's questions I let her make me up a pack of meat sandwiches, cake and lemonade. It was two o'clock in the morning by the time I was walking down the drive and the moon was almost as bright as the night before. The walk to Abergavenny took more than three hours, with no chance of a lift at that hour of the morning, so I had plenty of time for thinking.

Brigadier Moss was assuming that the shot into the conservatory and the grenade attack were connected with Keyson's death. It seemed a reasonable assumption. If so, my three fellow conspirators, Hal Hunter, Jack Kelso and David, along with Robin Duncan, were all strong suspects. But it puzzled me that these first two attempts – if they had been attempts – were so inefficient compared with the final shot that despatched Keyson. The conservatory bullet had missed Keyson by at least ten feet, probably more, the grenade by a wider margin. In both cases there'd been a considerable risk of killing somebody else by mistake, Stanley Gorton and Dr Stroud in the conservatory, Dr Stroud again with the grenade. In fact, up to the time that Keyson was found dead you could have argued that Dr Stroud was the real target. We had to assume that somebody wanted so much to take Colonel Keyson's life that he or she was prepared to kill an innocent man in the process.

Not a soul stirred as I walked down the white valley road, past the gates of farms folded away in the curves of the hills. Even at that hour warmth was still rising from the earth, drawing up with it smells of scorched grass, of meadowsweet, of water from the stream that ran alongside the road. I passed Monica Minter's house, where not a light was showing, and the turning to the Williams' farm at Cymyoy, imagining poor Gwenda lying awake and thinking of her lover on his way back to France. It was full light before I got to Abergavenny. I settled in a field outside the little town and made a picnic of Jenny's sandwiches and lemonade, waiting till I could see a few people up and about, then strolled through the town and up the hill towards the railway station.

The first thing I noticed was a bicycle, propped against the station wall. It had a dusty and abandoned air and looked to me very like the one Robin had taken from the shed the night before. I went up for a closer look, checking to see that nobody was watching me, and felt almost sure it was. He'd managed at least to complete the first stage of his journey.

Inside the station a young clerk was just raising the blind over the ticket window. His thick glasses and the slight nervous tic round his mouth showed why he'd managed to escape conscription.

'I'm sorry to bother you. Were you on duty this time yesterday morning?'

He nodded, looking scared.

'Do you remember if a young red-headed man with a Scottish accent bought a ticket?'

He shook his head, then had trouble stopping the shake. It didn't occur to him to ask why I wanted to know. He was just scared that he might have done something wrong.

'You don't remember, or he didn't?'

'No. He d . . . d . . . didn't.'

A stutter too, poor lad.

'Did you see anybody young and red-haired?'

Another vehement shake of the head. I thanked him and turned away. There was an old man standing by the door, grey-bearded and bleary eyed, in an overcoat tied up with baler twine. He followed me into the sunshine mumbling something about being an old soldier. If he had been, it must have been in the Boer War. I ignored him, strolled back to the town centre to buy a local paper then returned to the station. My plan, as far as I had one, was to question the porter when he came on duty.

As I came round the corner to the station I saw something that stopped me in my tracks. Two men in khaki uniform were standing outside the Great Western Hotel opposite. They wore red caps and were staring at people coming in and out of the station. Military police. Since it seemed unlikely that they carried out routine patrols in a little place like Abergavenny, it must mean that the hunt for Robin Duncan had started in earnest. I walked past them as casually as I could, wishing them a civil good morning and getting one in return. The bicycle was still there against the wall. They weren't concerned about it, but more alert hunters might be. I grabbed it by its handlebars and wheeled it into the booking hall.

'I want to send my bicycle by train, please.'

'Where t . . . t . . . to?'

'Oh, Hereford.'

It would do as well as anywhere. At least it wasn't on the main route for Moscow. A ticket was handed over, a label produced and tied to the handlebars. I wheeled it onto the platform just as the Hereford train was arriving and delivered it into the hands of the guard. As I watched the train carrying it away I reflected that I'd just added aiding a deserter to my other sins.

After that it was quiet on the platform for a while, except for a single engine taking on water and getting up steam. I read the local paper and found the report I needed to answer one of my questions. It was headed: 'Abergavenny women Pledge Support for our Fighting Men'.

'The well known patriotic speaker, Mrs Monica Minter, gave a stirring address to the Abergavenny branch of the Duty and Discipline Movement on Thursday, on the theme: "What can Women do for the War Effort?" A salad lunch was provided and a silver collection taken, amounting to four pounds eleven shillings and sixpence towards comforts for the troops. Afterwards the ladies spent the afternoon knitting socks for fighting men, while the Misses Price played selections from Gilbert and Sullivan on the piano.'

It added that Mrs Minter would be addressing a rally in Swansea on Saturday – that evening.

If I'd been tempted to doubt Monica Minter's alibi for the grenade, that doubt was now removed. And if I assumed, as Brigadier Moss did, that all three attacks were connected, that should clear her of the other two as well. I wasn't satisfied. I sat there staring at the paper until I was aware of somebody standing beside me. It was the old man from the booking hall. I was ready to snap at him to go away, thinking he was begging again, when he spoke.

'I seen him.'

'Who?'

'The young man you was asking about. I seen him yesterday.'

I grabbed his coat and pulled him down on the bench beside me.

'What did he look like?'

'Like you said, blazing red hair and in a blazing hurry too. Carrying a heavy great pack.'

'What time?'

'Earlier than this. It was before the station opened. He came up to me and asked when did it open. So I told him and he said what time was the first train to the docks.'

'What docks?'

'That's what I asked him. He looked at me as if he didn't know what I was talking about. I told him there were Cardiff Docks and Newport Docks and Milford Haven

Docks and what one did he fancy?'

'What did he say?'

'He didn't say nothing for a while. Then I asked him if he was in some kind of trouble, so when he didn't answer I took it that he was and I said he might as well make for Milford Haven because it was further away and they'd go looking in the other places first.'

'But the clerk said he didn't buy a ticket.'

He spat on the platform.

'He didn't need no ticket. I told him how to hop on from the side furthest away from the platform, after the guard's got in and before the train starts moving. No trouble for a youngster like him. I told him to hide himself in the gentleman's until the train was just going, then I'd come and rattle the door.'

'And you did?'

'Course I did. I rattled, up he got and away he went. Why pay the railway company if you don't have to? They got enough anyway.'

He spat again.

I glanced along the platform. One of the military policemen was standing near the entrance and this time a sergeant was with him.

'Have you told anybody else?'

He shook his head.

'They'll probably ask you if you've seen him.'

He glanced at them, then away again.

'Never tell a red cap anything you don't have to.'

I rummaged in my bag and found a ten shilling note. No sooner had I got it between my fingers than it was away again, whisking into the pocket of his overcoat like a rabbit into a burrow.

'Thanks, lady.'

I strolled past the military policemen, back to the ticket window and, speaking loudly enough for them to overhear, bought a return ticket to Swansea, not wanting to mention the name of Milford Haven. The booking clerk's stutter was worse than before, so I guessed they'd been questioning him.

120

I got out of the train at Milford Haven to a smell of salt and seaweed in the air and seagulls wheeling over the platform. There were boxes of fish in ice stacked on the platform opposite and masts and funnels of ships crowding the sky. Outside the station the streets were bustling with men in army and naval uniforms and the long waterway was crowded with dozens of merchant ships, waiting to make up convoys. I heard a group of people speaking French with heavy Belgian accents and gathered from a poster for a charity concert that the place was a haven for refugees as well as shipping.

I had to wait for some time at the harbour office before I could find out what I wanted because there were men from merchant ships ahead of me needing information about the next convoy. I gathered that it was due to sail shortly under the protection of Royal Naval ships. As I waited I noticed several military policemen and had to tell myself not to be jumpy. It was natural that there should be military police around a busy docks. It didn't mean they were looking for Robin Duncan. When it was my turn I asked if there were any ships about to leave for Russia and was told no. Apparently the revolution had cut trade with Russia to almost nothing.

'Supposing I wanted to ship something to Russia?'

The man at the desk gave me an odd look.

'You'd need to send it to one of the Baltic ports and see what could be done from there. There's one going out for Stockholm on the next tide.'

He gave me directions and I followed them along a quay, past a line of fishing boats, picking my way over ropes and the severed heads of cod with seagulls fighting over them. The ship bound for Stockholm was small, her plates rusted. Two men on the quay were bundling things into a loading net, mattresses wrapped and stitched into hessian parcels, several tea chests, a roll of carpet. From the deck two seamen in dark trousers and smocks watched them dourly. I waited until the net rose into the air and was being gathered on board before I went up to the men on the quayside.

'Excuse me, are you from this ship?'

'No lady, thank God. We're just finishing loading her.'

The empty net landed with a thump beside us. I shouted up the rusty cliff of the ship's side to the men on deck.

'Excuse me, I'm looking for somebody.'

The man on the quay shook his head.

'No good speaking English to them, lady. The only thing they understand is "Look out", and then only after it's hit them.'

I tried again in German and this time got a response. The two men on deck looked at each other, then one of them said, also in German.

'Who are you looking for, please?'

'His name's Robin Duncan. A young man. Is he on board?'

'Wait please.'

The two men conferred, then the one who'd done the talking disappeared, leaving the other to keep watch on me. A man came out in a master's cap and jacket and shouted down to me in careful English:

'What is your business, please?'

I explained again about Robin Duncan.

'You are from his family?'

'Yes.'

Nantgarrew, I decided, was a substitute family.

'Wait please.'

The ship didn't run to gangways. Its master came down a steel ladder to the quay.

'Is he a young man with red hair?'

'Yes. When did he arrive?'

'He came here yesterday. He said he would work for nothing if we would take him to Stockholm. He is in trouble?'

'I'd like to speak to him, please.'

He looked at me, weighing me up, then pointed to the ladder with an apologetic gesture. He seemed a decent, cautious man wanting to act for the best. He came behind me while I negotiated the ladder as best I could, thankful for a sound head for heights. There were a nasty few seconds when I had to step off it and onto the deck, but I landed safely. The ship's engines were already running. The two men I'd spoken to were securing a canvas cover over a hatch. They looked at me curiously.

'Follow me, please.'

The master led the way down a companionway into a strong smell of fish. There was a squat, unclean man standing at a table with a filleting knife. Behind him, bent over a large tub, was the red head of Robin Duncan. When he saw me the potato he'd been holding shot out of his hand half-peeled and back into the tub.

'What the bloody hell are you doing here?'

I fancied, perhaps unfairly, that part of his fury came from being discovered at the womanly task of peeling potatoes.

The master said to me: 'You must not be long. We sail in one hour's time.'

With or without their new galley hand, was the implication. He went back up the companionway. There was silence, apart from the wet whittle of the cook's knife through fish.

'I'm not coming back. You can say what you bloody like, I'm not coming back.'

I said: 'The military police are looking for you. You shouldn't have left the bicycle at Abergavenny station.'

'Bloody hell.'

He'd looked pale and strained at Nantgarrew but now he looked even worse, as if he hadn't slept for two nights, and still pathetically young. Looking at him, I thought the master might have decided he was my son. I was adding to the strain by letting him think the authorities were hotter on his trail than they were, but I needed a lever.

'The question is, what we're going to do about it. Can we talk here?'

I glanced at the cook, who seemed to be taking no notice of us.

'Don't worry about him. He doesn't speak English. None of them does, but for the captain.'

I caught the whiff of fear and loneliness from him,

stronger than the smell of fish. When he'd dreamed of going to join the revolution he hadn't imagined that it would be in a rusty hulk, peeling potatoes, with nobody to talk to.

There was a wooden chair jammed against the stove, broken-backed and sequinned with dried fish scales. I pulled it up beside the tub of potatoes and sat down. Mechanically, he went on peeling and gouging.

'Why did you leave Nantgarrew in such a hurry?'

'Why do you think?'

'I'm asking you.'

'You know why.'

'Was it because you'd just killed Colonel Keyson?'

'What?'

He stared at me, knife in one hand, potato in the other, face quite blank.

'He's killed?'

'He was shot not long before you put a gun to my head and cycled off.'

He stared at me for a long time, then the blankness gave way to his usual manner, just on the edge of insolence.

'Then good luck to the man who shot him.'

'Was it you?'

'Why are you asking me?'

'Because if it was you and you tell me so, it might save somebody else from being accused of it.'

'Oh, I see. That's the tune, is it? Come back Robin, be a man, confess and take your punishment. No thank you, Miss Bray.'

'Does that mean you did it?'

'What would you do if I told you I did?'

'That would depend.'

'Depend on what?'

'If you gave me a signed confession that you'd done it, a full and signed confession that could be produced in court, I might agree to hold it until I knew you were safely in Russia.'

From Russia, in its present ferment, he was never likely to be extradited, even if he survived the revolution he was so determined to reach.

'Oh aye. And the alternative?'

'The alternative is that I tell the ship's master you're an army deserter and alert the police at the dock gates before the ship sails.'

He thought about it for the space of one potato, a potato more carefully peeled than any in that ship's galley was likely to have been before. When he'd pared it quite nude he stared at it as if it had the answer.

'Well, you're a clever woman, Miss Bray. I tell you the truth about what I did to Colonel Ralph Keyson and in return you agree to let me go. Is that it?'

'Yes. But it has to be a written confession.'

He slid the potato into a huge saucepan on top of the others.

'Have you got a pen and paper with you?'

I had a pen. There was a greasy order book on a shelf. The cook didn't even bother to look round as I tore out its blank middle pages. I put the book on the draining board so that Robin had it to rest his confession on and offered him the backless chair, but he wrote standing up. It didn't take him long and what he wrote took up less than one side of a sheet of paper. He passed it to me. It was neatly and firmly written, considering the circumstances, and signed with a flourish. It read:

'I, Robin Duncan, do hereby freely and unreservedly confess that I played no part in the justified assassination of the military mass murderer known as Colonel Ralph Keyson of the British imperialist army. In failing to take any share in this action, I am guilty of neglecting my duty as a man of the people. Signed Robin Duncan, in the presence of Miss Nell Bray.' He'd dated it and left a space for my signature.

I looked at him. He was grinning.

'Well, aren't you going to sign it?'

'You're telling me you didn't kill him?'

'You've read it, but if you want me to say it: No, I did not kill Ralph Keyson.'

'When that grenade exploded, you said you didn't throw

it. Did you have anything else to do with it?'

He whistled a couple of notes. Writing the confession had put some confidence back into him.

'That's not playing fair. You're trying to get something else from the bargain after it's made.'

'Did you?'

'Well, I'll give it to you as a luck penny. No, I did not. The last grenade I had in my hand I threw at some poor bloody German fellow-worker. The same goes for the last shot I fired.'

He picked up his knife, selected a large potato from the tub and went back to his peeling. I read the confession again.

'Do you know who did it?'

He didn't turn round.

'That's no part of the bargain.'

'Did you steal one of Jack Kelso's revolvers?'

'Nor is that, but you can tell Jack from me not to worry, it will be doing good service on the barricades in Moscow.'

He was becoming positively cheerful. I think, after a tense and silent day on the ship, it was doing him good to talk to somebody he knew.

'When you were cycling away from Nantgarrew, did you meet anybody on the road?'

There was no immediate answer to that. He must have peeled half a potato before he said anything.

'No, I did not.'

This was crucial to the truth of his story, or Jenny's. According to Jenny, she'd seen Mrs Minter ride away downhill on a bicycle some time before the shot was fired, run after her, sprained her ankle and limped back uphill to Nantgarrew. Mrs Minter – if she'd ever been there in the first place – could have been safely home before Robin set out, but he could hardly have missed seeing Jenny on her slow and painful return journey.

'What became of your puttees? You might find those useful on the barricades too.'

'What are you talking about?'

'Your puttee came in useful for bandaging Jenny

Chesney's ankle, or part of it did.'

He turned round.

'If she told you about it, why ask me?'

'It was your puttee, then?'

He nodded.

'So you did meet Jenny?'

'I don't know why you're trying to trick me. Yes, I met Jenny Chesney, if you can call it meeting.'

'You said you didn't meet anybody on the road.'

'I wasn't going to get her into trouble.'

'Why would you get her into trouble?'

'For not trying to stop me. I thought that was what she was at, when I ran into her, trying to stop me, but it wasn't that at all.'

I said: 'I think you'd better tell me what happened.'

It was half an hour since we'd begun talking and there were shouts and bangs overhead as the hatches were battened down. Another half hour and the ship would be sailing, the decision made one way or another. Because of this, I think, he dropped his sarcastic tone and told his story quite simply, but in a puzzled way as if he still didn't understand it himself.

'I was pedalling hard downhill, then I saw this person – man or woman, I didn't know which it was – on the road ahead of me. When I got nearer, I could see it was a woman. I couldn't see her face so I thought it was the mad besom . . . '

'But wasn't she walking towards you?'

'She was not. She was walking away from me. Then when she heard the bicycle she turned round and stepped straight out into the road in front of me. I ran into her. I couldn't help it. That's how her ankle got hurt.'

This, however puzzling, had the sound of truth to me. There seemed no reason for Robin to make it up. Yet Jenny, by her account, had been running downhill when she tripped and hurt her ankle.

'Was she trying to stop you?'

'That was what I thought. But when I put the bicycle down and went over to find out how badly hurt she was, she was surprised it was me. She hadn't known till then.'

'How do you know?'

'She said so. She looked terrified out of her mind, then she gave a gasp and said "Oh Robin, it's you." Then she said she was sorry she'd jumped in front of me. She thought I was somebody else.'

'Who else?'

'I didn't ask her. She was trembling and crying and I was busy doing up her ankle.'

'She knew you were running away?'

'She must have. I asked her not to say anything till morning to give me a chance. She promised.'

A rope thudded on the deck over our heads. The engines throbbed. The cook wiped his hands on his thighs and went up the companionway without looking at us. I heard shouts from the quay.

Robin said: 'We'll be sailing any minute now. You'll need to go ashore.'

I looked at him, at the confession lying on the draining board, blotched now with dirty water. One thing turned the scales. Does a man running away from a murder stop to bandage somebody's ankle? Goodness knows. The scales wavered, weighted down by the merest hair. He hadn't denied stealing Jack Kelso's gun. I held out my hand to him.

'Good luck, Mr Duncan. I hope the revolution doesn't prove a disappointment to you.'

Surprise and relief showed on his face for a second, then he shook my hand.

'It can't be more of a disappointment than what there's been so far.'

The captain called from the top of the companionway. I dare say he'd forgotten till that moment that I was there.

'Madam, you must go now. We are sailing.'

He waited and, as I came up on deck, registered that Robin wasn't with me.

'Thank you, Captain. May I wish you a safe voyage.'

Relieved that there was no family row to deal with, he escorted me briskly to the gap in the rails. Going down the ladder was worse than coming up it, but at least it was a distraction from my thoughts about Jenny.

I stood on the quay and watched as the last cable was coiled on board and a gap of water appeared between the ship and the land. There was no sign of Robin on deck. His parting would be marked by potato peelings, not poetry. One of the dockers was standing beside me.

'You found your friend then. All right, is he?'

'I hope so.'

But what about the other friend? Who had she expected to see on the valley road in the moonlight and why hadn't she told me? The gap of water was widening. A tug whistled and the ship turned its broad rusty stern towards us. Right or wrong, it was too late now.

FIFTEEN

IT WAS WORRY ABOUT JENNY that made me decide to attend Monica Minter's patriotic rally in Swansea. I couldn't go back to Nantgarrew until I had at least tried to answer some of the questions about her story, and the vital one was whether Monica Minter really had been near Nantgarrew on the night Keyson died. I had the idea, too, that I might learn more about Monica Minter watching her among her own kind. I took the train to Swansea and reserved a bed for the night at a boarding house in a side street, kept by a young, care-worn woman with several children. A faded red circle in the window read 'Not at Home. A Man from this House Is Now Serving in His Majesty's Forces'. The woman's enthusiasm for the war seemed to have faded along with the notice, judging from the expression on her face when she directed me to the hall where the patriotic rally was taking place.

But there were still plenty of people in Swansea solid for the war. There must have been eight hundred or so seats in the hall and most of them were filled within minutes of the doors opening. I chose a seat in the middle of the second row from the back, wanting to hear her in action without being noticed. There were a table and four chairs on the platform, a line of Allied flags pinned to the wall behind them with an enormous Union Jack in the centre. A banner across the front of the platform announced, in letters of red and gold: 'Women of Wales support our Heroes'. A programme sheet being circulated along the rows announced four speakers: a local councillor who was acting as chairman, then Mrs Monica Minter of the Duty and Discipline Movement, a Wounded Officer recently invalided home from the Front and a Conservative MP.

As the chairman orated about glorious sacrifice and the imminence of victory I had to remind myself that this time I wasn't there to heckle. The audience heard him politely and applauded, but there was a perceptible increase in excitement when Mrs Minter got to her feet. I noticed that she was cool and experienced enough to use the wave of applause that greeted her, launching herself on it before it quite died away. She stood there, a tall and imposing figure in her boots, her black skirt and tightly belted red jacket, a red and black tricorn hat on her dark hair, as vivid and confident as the Union Jack behind her.

At first she gave them exactly what I'd expected, the courage of our men in the trenches, the brave sacrifices of mothers, wives and sisters at home, the reminder that she was speaking as one whose brother had made the supreme sacrifice, whose husband was serving in the North Sea. The audience loved it and I saw several women in tears, but I sensed an expectation that there was more and better to come. The voice that had been talking in hushed tones about sacrifice became louder and more aggressive.

'Another part of our duty here at home, Mr Chairman, ladies and gentlemen, is to silence those voices of defeat, those enemy agents in our midst who dare to tell us that these sacrifices have no value, that our cause is no longer a just one. We must give those voices of defeat no quarter, just as our husbands, our brothers, our sons give no quarter to the enemy in the field. The highest part of our duty at home is to root out treason in whatever forms it comes. And, ladies and gentlemen, it comes in some very strange forms indeed.'

Another change of voice now, confiding, almost arch. Her audience shifted, making itself comfortable in anticipation of a treat. She had placed a square leather bag on the table in front of her, like a music case. She delved into it, smiling at us like somebody about to perform a conjuring trick. Her hand emerged holding a sheaf of typescript. I felt a prickling in my skin, an awareness of oncoming trouble.

'Here, ladies and gentlemen, I have a very curious report. It's a medical document, of a kind. A record of the treatment given by an officer in the Royal Army Medical Corps to an officer recently sent home from France, allegedly as a victim of a war wound. The officer is referred to in this report as Mr Bird, which for reasons which will become obvious to you is . . . I was going to say a *nom de guerre*, but in the circumstances it seems hardly appropriate. I propose to read you an extract from that report.' She lowered her voice, looked round the audience. 'And I must apologise to you in advance for some passages which any decent person will naturally find offensive.'

By then she had them in the palm of her hand. There seems, goodness knows why, to be a general pleasure in prying into other people's medical details. To be invited to do so in the name of patriotism, with a hint of scandal to come, was strawberries and cream to her audience. She paused for effect, shuffled the typed pages and began to read.

' "Notes of two hour session with Mr Bird, May 27. Mr Bird now shares my view that his repression is likely to result from unacknowledged sexual impulse towards his mother." ' There was a gasp from the front row. Mrs Minter threw a stern look in its direction and read on. ' "Described dream of previous night in which beautiful woman wearing light dress was standing over him urging him to eat large bowlful of sherry trifle. Remembers there were raspberries in trifle." ' Mrs Minter looked up. 'There's a note in brackets which I admit is not entirely clear to me: "Possibly raspberries equal nipples, recollection of first infantile oral satisfaction now denied to patient." ' She ignored the gasps and a few giggles, soon hushed. ' "Patient interested in my suggestion that woman represented his mother. Asked if he had any memory of seeing his mother and father making love." '

Commotion in the front row. A large woman in black struggled to her feet and walked out, followed by a small man. The chairman called for order. Mrs Minter waited

for the buzz to die down and read on, unflurried.
' "Patient at first denied it, but denials clearly related to later phallic stage of libido. When pressed by me to recall earlier stage, recounted memory at age of two or thereabouts. Crawled from nursery onto landing and conscious of some event behind half opened door of parents' bedroom. Claims he is unable to recall nature of event, but I suspect repression. But did experience sudden vivid recollection of being picked up by his mother (query, in her nightdress?), taken back to bed and fed 'warm milk and paps', patient's own very significant name for bread and milk. Terminated session at this point. Strongest support so far for tentative diagnosis of schizophrenia owing to repression of Oedipal urges at oral stage of sexual development. Urged patient to write down tonight's dream immediately on waking. Further session tomorrow morning." '

The audience was quiet now, entranced by its own sense of outrage, and in such a respectable cause too. Clearly pleased with the effect she'd made, Monica Minter laid the typescript down on top of her bag and leaned forward. There was more to come. Her voice was so hushed that it seemed scarcely above a normal speaking tone, but it carried perfectly to the back of the hall.

'And that, ladies and gentlemen, is how a doctor holding His Majesty's Commission in the Royal Army Medical Corps treats a patient who tried to murder a comrade in arms in the trenches.'

Uproar. Boos and hisses welled up from the crowd. Several men in the front rows were standing up waving their fists. It would have looked as if they were waving them at the tall, upright figure of Monica Minter, until you saw the expression on her face. Self-controlled as she was, she couldn't keep back the smile of a speaker who has her audience exactly where she wants it. The chairman realised it was useless even trying to restore order until the audience had expressed its feelings. For what seemed like long minutes Monica Minter smiled, the crowd stamped and shouted and I sat there wondering where this left us.

When there was enough quiet for her to start again she rounded off her efforts with a denunciation of the alien Dr Sigmund Freud and all his works. She stopped just short of giving Nantgarrew's location and leading the crowd off to attack it. If she'd invited them to do it I think they'd have passed a resolution to dismantle it stone by stone. But we were left in no doubt of her opinion of cowards who tried to evade their lawful service or the German-inspired so-called doctors who encouraged them to do it with obscene talk about dreams and raspberries. She rested her case and sat down to a storm of applause.

After that even the speech by the Wounded Officer came as an anti-climax. I let his manly platitudes wash over me and thought. There could be no doubt that the patient referred to as Mr Bird was Stanley Gorton. That, and what I'd heard from Jenny about Dr Stroud's methods, left me in no doubt that the report was genuine. Little doubt either that it was one of the reports stolen from Dr Stroud's filing cabinet that had caused Jenny such distress. That left two questions: how it had come into Mrs Minter's hands and whether she was right when she claimed that Stanley Gorton had attempted murder. If so, how did she know that? I watched her as she listened to the wounded officer and stowed the report away in her big leather bag. The eyes of the audience followed it like children's following sweets. I wanted to get my hands on that typescript. I needed to prove that it was part of the batch stolen from Nantgarrew. The question of how to do it lasted me through most of the bellicose speech by the Conservative MP. By the time the audience was streaming into the evening sunshine, still in a state of excitement from Monica Minter's speech, I'd worked out a plan.

It depended on the fact that speakers are always reluctant to leave the scene of their triumphs. I knew I could count on Mrs Minter and the rest of the platform party lingering to accept congratulations. Being close to the back of the hall I was one of the first out, and almost immediately I saw what I needed. Three lads, perhaps twelve or thirteen years old, were lingering on the steps outside sniggering at the people coming out, shouting the occasional rude remark. They had one bottle of ginger beer between them and were passing it from hand to hand, taking carefully measured swigs with a great show of bravado. Their boots and collars looked as if some large animal had chewed them, their faces were smeared with jam and dust. I went up to the tallest of them, as unobtrusively as possible.

'Do you want to earn half a crown?'

His eyes narrowed.

'Between us or each?'

'Each.'

It was no time for penny pinching.

'Doing what?'

'Come round the corner and I'll tell you.'

My disreputable allies followed me round the corner. I described Mrs Minter to them and produced from my bag a few of the leaflets I always carry with me, setting out the case for ending the war.

'She'll be coming out in a few minutes. There'll probably be some other people with her. When you see her, shout 'Stop the slaughter', throw some of these leaflets in front of her then run as fast as you can. You'll have to look lively. She's probably a good sprinter.'

It was meat and drink to them. They didn't even look at the leaflets and, at half a crown a go, didn't mind what they shouted. I gave them their money, saw them off to their posts on the steps then stood just round the corner of the building, craning my neck for a view of the front of the hall. It was just as well I hadn't wasted any time because within a few minutes Mrs Minter, along with the MP and the wounded officer, came out of the main doors.

My mercenaries played their part almost perfectly. It's true that the smallest one, carried away by excitement, shouted 'Bugger the Kaiser' instead of 'Stop the Slaughter', but I wasn't concerned about the politics of the thing. What I wanted was the leather bag and my chances of getting it depended on how well I'd read Monica Minter's character. In the event, she reacted just as I'd hoped. She caught one of the leaflets in mid-air, glanced at it, uttered a yell of rage and went off at a run after the biggest boy who was already haring across the road, in between the motor cars and delivery carts. Volleys of hoots and curses from the drivers followed him as he went, then started up again for Mrs Minter, running a good fifty yards behind him. As I'd hoped, she put down her bag before she gave chase, trusting it, I suppose, to the care of her companions. But the officer was already away in pursuit of the second boy and the MP, after some indecision, went half-heartedly on the track of the third. The leather bag was left sitting there and it took only a few strides from my corner to grab it. Nobody saw me. Everybody was too busy watching the escape of the boys or tut-tutting over my leaflets. I walked rapidly down a side street away from the hall, carrying my prize, and found a small park with a secluded bench behind a shrubbery.

I found the typescript almost at once, along with pages of notes for her speech. The passages she'd read out were marked in red ink but there were several pages more, all of them relating to 'Mr Bird'. They were almost exclusively concerned with more of his dreams and their interpretation, with no reference at all to attempted murder. Two handwritten pages were clipped to the typescript and seemed to be later case notes by Dr Stroud, probably the ones that Jenny had not yet got round to typing. There were symbols and abbreviations I didn't understand and the handwriting was difficult, but I could make out that the notes related to Stanley Gorton's condition over the past week. There was a reference to an argument with another patient over breakfast – obviously Ralph Keyson. A sentence at the top of the first page was underlined. 'Serious regression resulting initially from trauma from malicious practical joke by fellow patient.' The date on that entry was three days before I'd arrived at Nantgarrew, the day of the shooting incident in the conservatory. This suggested that Dr Stroud knew more about that incident than he'd been prepared to tell me. But still, nothing about Stanley Gorton's attempted murder.

The next few pages of typescript were clearly part of Dr Stroud's book. They were headed, 'Preliminary observations on the use of psychoanalysis in cases of combat neurosis'. I skimmed through them and found nothing of interest. Then another batch of pages, handwritten like Stanley Gorton's later notes. The word 'murder' leapt out at me from the first page. 'Subject experienced great calm once murder decided upon as course of action. Some initial reluctance to use word "murder" gradually overcome. Total concentration on detail of the act, to the exclusion of wider implications . . .'

So Monica Minter had been right. Stanley Gorton had attempted to commit a murder. Jenny had hinted at it, but wouldn't tell me outright. As for Dr Stroud, of course he wouldn't tell me anything. He must have been sitting there, hour after hour, with Stanley Gorton on his couch, probing into the emotions and motivations of it without giving anybody else a hint of how it might affect what was happening at Nantgarrew. After that initial surprise, the notes were unrevealing. What seemed to puzzle Dr Stroud was that once the subject had decided on his course of murder, his dreams had ceased entirely. Repression was the verdict. Patient sublimating repressed sexual urges in obsessively detailed plans for violent act. Well, all that might be of great interest to Dr Stroud, but it didn't interest me. What I wanted to know was who Stanley Gorton had tried to murder and how he'd tried to do it.

I stowed the whole batch of documents away in my own bag, then noticed a letter on the ground beside me. It must have fallen out of Mrs Minter's bag when I took the papers out. I picked it up, intending to restore it. It was no part of my business to read her private mail. But the signature caught my eye. It was a name that had been very much on my mind over the past few days. The name was Ralph Keyson. My first throught was that Mrs Minter must have stolen that from Nantgarrew too. Then I saw that it began, 'My dear Mrs Minter . . .'

I glanced at the top of the page. The address was simply

'Somewhere in France'. The date was almost a year ago, July 1916.

'My dear Mrs Minter,
    I heard the news today and am writing to express my heartfelt sympathy with you in your great loss. As you know, your brother and I were at school together. I have always felt the greatest respect and affection for him. You have lost a devoted brother, and I a very good friend. I know you well enough to be sure that you will find consolation in the fact that he died bravely, doing his duty. My thoughts are with you. Perhaps when I am next home on leave I may be permitted to call on you again and talk about Simon. For now, please accept my most sincere sympathy.
            Yours sincerely,
            Ralph Keyson'

I sat there amazed, the letter in my hand. I'd had no indication from anybody that Monica Minter knew Ralph Keyson. If anybody at Nantgarrew knew, he or she had said nothing about it, which was surely strange with her name cropping up so often. Yet the letter suggested a friendship of long-standing. He spoke of calling on her 'again' so he'd been a visitor to her home at least once in the past. Had she known he was one of the patients at Nantgarrew and, if so, how could she have brought herself to brand them all as cowards with a friend of her dead brother among them?

Unless she really was mad and sorrow for her brother had so unbalanced her mind that she resented any friend of his who'd survived. In that case, was Ralph Keyson the centre of her attack? She had a revolver and said she was prepared to use it. But she couldn't have thrown the grenade into the study. I'd proved that.

It was turning to dusk. A man was coming with keys, letting me know he was about to lock the park gates. I put the letter back into Mrs Minter's bag and, carrying it in one hand, my own bag in the other, let him usher me out to the street.

The next problem was getting the bag, deprived of its stolen pages, back to Monica Minter. I was building up enough charges against myself without adding petty theft. My original plan had been to take it back to the hall where the meeting was held and leave it there for somebody to discover. But on my way I saw the familiar sight of Mrs Minter's red motor car, parked outside one of the city's most prominent hotels. That made my job easier. I simply strolled past and, without stopping, dropped the bag in front of the passenger seat. I was reasonably sure that nobody had seen me but paused on the next corner to look back. At that moment Mrs Minter came out of the hotel and down the steps towards her motor car.

Luckily she wasn't looking in my direction, too busy talking to the two men with her. One was the officer who'd spoken at the meeting. The other, though dressed in civilian clothes and bowler hat, still contrived to walk as if he were wearing cavalry boots and spurs. It was none other than the man who'd questioned me the day before at Nantgarrew, Brigadier Moss. Even from this distance, it was clear he was still in a bad temper. He and Mrs Minter had halted on the bottom step, looking at each other. She said something, made an angry gesture. He stepped back and brought his heels together as if about to bark an order, probably to have her clapped in the guard room by the look of it. She seemed unmoved. He glared, said something short and sharp, then turned and walked off, in the opposite direction from where I was standing.

Monica Minter said something to the officer and shrugged. The hotel doorman followed them across the pavement to her motor car and began to crank the starting handle. The officer held the driver's door open for her and she tied on her motoring hat, adjusted her goggles and climbed in. He walked round to the passenger's side. His feet must have made contact with the bag as soon as he sat down and he held it up for her to see. She snatched it from him and began to search through it. The car started but she yelled to the poor doorman to stop cranking as if it were his fault. At that point I decided to remove myself from the scene and made my way back to my boarding house, taking with me another question. What in the world could Monica Minter have done to make Brigadier Moss so angry with her?

SIXTEEN

IT TOOK MOST OF THE next day to get back to Nantgarrew. They were just sitting down to Sunday supper as I arrived, foot-sore and hungry. Neither staff nor patients looked any happier than when I'd last seen them. Dr Stroud and Dr Caspian both seemed deathly tired. Jenny kept glancing at me, almost saying something then biting her lip and looking away.

David said: 'Evening Nell, had a nice trip?' in a deliberately provoking tone that suggested I'd been off to the seaside with bucket and spade. Hal Hunter ignored me as usual. Jack Kelso, unusually subdued, busied himself seeing that my plate was filled with salad and corned beef. Stanley Gorton, sitting beside me, managed to combine a mumble of greeting with a suspicious look, as if he expected me to steal from his plate.

This look, which normally would have amused me, made me shudder. I looked down at his hands, busy with knife and fork. They were plump and pale, blotched with spreading freckles, sprouting harsh hairs. I looked away and found Jenny's eyes on me again. Nobody seemed inclined to linger over the meal. As they queued at the urn for coffee I went over to Dr Stroud.

'I need to speak to you.'

He nodded and led the way across the hall to a study smaller than his own. From the complicated charts on the wall and a shiny horse-hair couch, I took it to be Dr Caspian's consulting room.

I said: 'I've found your records, the ones that were stolen.'

141

I took the pages of typescript and manuscript out of my bag and put them on the desk in front of him. He looked from them to me and back again. I guessed that it was part of his professional technique never to look surprised, but he was having to struggle to hold on to it.

'Where did you find them?'

'Mrs Minter had them. I'm afraid she quoted from them at a big rally in Swansea.'

He flinched and put a hand to his head.

'What did she quote?'

'Stanley Gorton's dream about the trifle. It's the passage marked in red.'

He found the place and read, slowly.

'Was that all?'

'It seemed enough. Yes, that was all she quoted. But she said something else about him.'

'What?'

'She said the patient you called Mr Bird had tried to murder another soldier in the trenches.'

He stared at me.

'Is that true?'

'Yes. Heaven knows how that woman found out about it, but it's true.'

'What happened?'

He started to protest, but I cut him short.

'Doctor, if you're going to plead professional confidence, it's a waste of time. There were eight hundred people in that hall and an MP with her on the platform.'

He groaned.

'Anyway, I assume the authorities knew about it. Brigadier Moss, for instance?'

'Oh yes, he knew. He didn't want Gorton sent here in the first place, but he was overruled.'

'Well then, what happened?'

'He had an argument with another officer and tried to kill him.'

'An argument about food, by any chance?'

'Yes, apparently he accused another lieutenant in his dug-out of taking more than his fair share of biscuits.'

142

'So he tried to kill a man over some biscuits?'

'I think you've heard enough, Miss Bray, to understand that it wasn't really about biscuits. I believe I'm close to bringing him to accept that he unconsciously saw the lieutenant as an infant rival for his mother's breasts.'

'How did he try to kill him?'

He shifted uneasily in his chair.

'It seems to have been some form of booby trap.'

'What kind?'

'He'd wedged a hand grenade inside a biscuit tin with a weight on top of it. I think the idea was that if the other man really had been trying to steal biscuits the grenade would have gone off when he moved the tin.'

It was my turn to stare. I could hardly believe what I was hearing.

'A grenade? Why in heaven's name didn't you tell me about this?'

'Frankly, Miss Bray, why should I? You aren't here in any official capacity.'

I practically shouted at him.

'What's that got to do with it? I'm trying to help you, but you're treating me as if I were the enemy.'

'I appreciate that you want to help. But in any case, I can't see the relevance of this.'

'Relevance? When a grenade goes off in your study? When a man's shot dead the day after he had an argument about food with Stanley Gorton? Is there something about psychology that destroys common sense?'

'I can understand why you're angry . . . '

If he'd told me that it was because I was repressing my unconscious I think I'd have thrown a paper-weight at him. Luckily he didn't.

' . . . but I don't think it would have helped if you had known. Are you suggesting that Gorton threw a grenade through my window or shot Colonel Keyson?'

I wasn't. The facts remained that Gorton could hardly have got from the road to the study window in time to throw the grenade, or from the kitchen to the barbed wire fence in time to shoot Keyson.

143

'I'm not suggesting anything yet, but I do think you might trust me. I've already conspired to confuse the evidence in a murder case and aided a deserter to escape. What more do you expect?'

'Aided a deserter? You found Robin Duncan?'

I told him about it, including the fact that his bicycle was now standing on a station platform at Hereford. He seemed relieved to know that Robin was already beyond the reach of Brigadier Moss. I pointed out that failure to recapture him would hardly improve Brigadier Moss's temper.

'That's past praying for in any case.'

'Did he come back while I was away?'

'No. We've been left alone.'

'I suppose he was busy elsewhere. I saw him in Swansea talking to Mrs Minter.'

'I might have known he'd be hand-in-glove with that woman.'

'I'm not so sure. From what I could see, they were having an argument.'

'I imagine that she was urging him to close us down out of hand.'

A fat white moth fluttered outside the window. I felt tired after my long walk and my anger, and sorry for Dr Stroud, who looked so much more tired.

'Dr Stroud, do you know how Brigadier Moss got to hear about that argument between Ralph Keyson and David Ellward?'

He shook his head.

'I wish I did. He asked you about that too, did he? He seems unreasonably interested in it.'

'I don't think we've managed to convince him that Ralph Keyson shot himself, do you?'

He was silent for a long time, then:

'Goodness knows.'

'What about the grenade? Does he know about the two that were stolen from Jack Kelso?'

'Yes. That came out, I'm afraid. Brigadier Moss sent a man up from Newport to take away Jack's collection. Jack's a little depressed about that, but I think I've persuaded Moss not to press charges against him. I said he should hold me responsible, and he does.'

He sighed. It would have been cruel to remind him that he'd originally been sceptical about the theft of the grenades. I said I was dog tired and wanted to go up to my room. We could talk again in the morning. I left him sitting there in the study, watching the moth.

As I'd expected, I'd hardly had time to take my shoes off and bathe my aching feet before there was a tap on the door and Jenny's urgent voice.

'Nell, may I come in?'

She came in as if escaping from somebody and stood just inside the door, staring at me with my feet in the washing bowl.

'Nell, I've been frantic. Where have you been? Did you find Robin?'

'Yes. He's all right, assuming the U-boats don't get him.'

'Thank God for that.'

'We had an interesting talk before his ship sailed.'

'What about?'

'About what you were doing that night Ralph Keyson was shot.'

She gasped as if I'd hit her.

'You'd better sit down.'

She sat on the edge of the chair, ankles together, hands clasped. Her eyes were big with tiredness. I looked at her and thought how little I really knew about her. In the past we'd marched together, attended demonstrations together. It hadn't seemed necessary to know more than that we both believed in the same cause. Since then Nantgarrew, or the war, or something else, had changed her.

'You can start by telling me the truth about what happened between you and Robin Duncan that night.'

She looked at me as if she thought her obvious misery would make me merciful, and saw she was wrong.

'I didn't tell anybody because I wanted him to get away. If I'd told anybody that night, they'd have had to try to bring him back.'

145

'Why did you want Robin to get away?'

'We were doing him no good here. He'd have gone anyway.'

'No other reason?'

She shook her head.

'Tell me exactly what happened.'

'I told you, I was running down the road after Mrs Minter when I fell and twisted my ankle. What I didn't tell you was that Robin found me and bandaged it for me.'

'He says you turned round and stepped out in front of him.'

'I didn't mean to. Only . . .'

'Only what?'

'I was so confused and scared.'

'What were you scared of?'

'Mrs Minter.'

'But you were chasing her. She was somewhere ahead of you.'

'I was still scared from seeing her. Then when I saw Robin coming I suppose I panicked.'

'You didn't know it was Robin at first?'

'No.'

'So who did you think it was?'

'What do you mean?'

'Robin says you told him you thought he was somebody else. Who did you expect to see?'

'You.'

'Why me?'

'I thought you must have heard me and come out after me.'

It was a weak story and she knew it.

'What else haven't you told me? Did you know, for instance, that Ralph Keyson and Monica Minter were friends?

'No!'

There was no doubt that it shocked her.

'He wrote to commiserate with her when her brother was killed. Did he ever say anything to you about her?'

'No.'

'Another thing: on Friday, when Brigadier Moss was here, Jack Kelso came out of his interview with him in a great hurry to find you. Why was that?'

She wrinkled her forehead, as if she had to try hard to remember.

'I think he wanted to tell me that Brigadier Moss wanted to talk to me later.'

'Only that?'

'As far as I can remember.'

'But in the end he didn't talk to you later because of the panic over looking for Robin.'

'No.'

'You realise Brigadier Moss will be back?'

'You think so?'

'I'm sure. After all, a man's been shot.'

'But he killed himself. Why won't anybody believe that?'

I looked at her.

'Do you believe it? If so, you're probably the only person here who does.'

She looked as if I'd hit her. I remembered that I must make allowances for the fact that she'd been close to the man, perhaps had even loved him. Angry though I was, I tried to go gently over dangerous ground.

'Brigadier Moss will want to speak to you, and I'm afraid that somehow he seems to know quite a lot about what's been happening here.'

'Yes.'

She wouldn't look at me.

'He's the kind of man who'd take a very censorious attitude to the kind of relationship that you and I might not regard as wrong.'

'Like poor Gwenda, you mean?'

'If you like.'

'What could he do about it?'

'I imagine at the very least he might send you away from Nantgarrew.'

'I don't have to talk to him. It's not as if I'm in the army.'

'It might not be sensible to refuse.'

'Sensible. It's gone a long way beyond that, I'm afraid,

Nell.'

She stood up.

'Sorry to have taken up your time. I'm glad Robin's all right, anyway.'

She managed to get out of the room without giving way, but a few seconds later I heard springs creak next door as if she'd thrown herself violently down on the bed.

I dried my feet and went over to open the window, needing air. From the common room below I heard voices and the sound of Tchaikovsky, well played on a mediocre piano. It was a favourite piece of David's. I leaned out of the window and the sight of the conservatory reminded me of a question I'd forgotten to ask Dr Stroud. What was the practical joke by a fellow officer that had so dismayed Stanley Gorton? In any case, I was almost certain I had the answer to that close to hand, but it would have to wait until daylight.

I stayed at the window in the dusk, breathing the scent of warm bracken from the hills and thinking of Mrs Minter. On the morning before the grenade went off, Hal Hunter claimed to have seen her close to Dr Stroud's study window. When I asked her later what she'd been doing there she said it had been a little surprise for us and told me to wait and see. But the grenade had exploded about six hours after her visit and, according to Jack Kelso, the maximum delay once the lever was released was seven seconds. She might possibly have set up some kind of booby trap device, but in that case why hadn't it exploded when the first patient of the day, Stanley Gorton, lay down on the couch?

I took the questions to bed with me, but sleep didn't answer them. I'd set my mind to wake up at five o'clock, but the sun woke me a little before that. I dressed quietly, so as not to wake Jenny, went downstairs and through the corridor to the inner door of the conservatory. The piece of bicycle inner tube that I'd found on the lawn the morning after the murder was in my pocket.

It was an odd feeling standing inside the conservatory and looking out at the shrubbery, thinking how Ralph

Keyson had stood there and stared at me four days before. The dark leaves of the rhododendrons hung heavy and motionless. It would have been easy to imagine somebody hidden by them, looking in. I turned away and looked for the geranium plants. The largest of them, a lanky father of many cuttings with a few yellowing leaves and bare stems, was in a big pot by the back wall, to the right of the door I'd come through. It needed watering and Ralph Keyson had been right about the infestation of white-fly. But my interest was in the soil of the pot. I knelt down for a close look at it and my heart jumped when I saw what I'd half expected to see: two small holes right at the back of the pot, going deep down into the dry soil.

I stood up and looked round for something that might fit the holes. There was a loose bundle of thin bamboo canes propped against the wall, meant for staking pot plants. I chose a pair of them about three feet long and pushed them into the holes of the geranium pot. They slid in so sweetly that any remaining doubt disappeared. I took the piece of cycle inner tube out of my pocket and wasn't at all surprised to find that there were small slits in the ends of it that fitted neatly over the canes. Slide it halfway down and there you have the simplest of weapons, the catapult. Once you have your catapult, it's more than flesh and blood can stand not to use it. Not a stone, I didn't want to break any more glass. I looked around and saw a trayful of daffodil bulbs left to dry. I picked a small rounded one, inserted it into my catapult, pulled back the inner tube and let fly. It plumped square against the glass of the new window pane, fell back, rolled along the floor. If it had grown into the finest daffodil ever cultivated I don't think it could have given me as much pleasure as it gave me then.

A knock at the window from outside. A face at the glass, mouthing at me. I just stopped myself from shouting out, then saw that it was the gardening boy, up early. I waved at him in what I hoped was a reassuring way, opened the outside door and let him in. He was more scared than I was.

SEVENTEEN

THE TWO BAMBOO STICKS AND the piece of inner tube were laid out on Dr Stroud's desk. We were back in his own study, with the couch gone and the walls and floor still bearing the marks of the grenade explosion.

I said: 'You accept what I say, that you must have known from the start?'

'I accept it.'

His voice was tired.

'He must have intended to take the catapult away before you saw it. But he had to pretend to look for a person with a gun, then pretend to discover the bullet in the wall. A bullet that he'd carefully lodged in a hole there before he got Gorton to go into the conservatory with him.'

'Yes, I suppose so.'

'It's the only thing that fits. He knew how suggestible Gorton was. He broke the window with a pebble from a catapult on the inside, while he was pretending to look at the geranium. Then he produced the bullet he'd planted and convinced the wretched man that somebody had been firing at him. I suppose it was meant to be revenge for Gorton's murder attempt on that soldier back in the trenches with the hand grenade. Because of course, Keyson would have heard all about that.'

'Yes. Unfortunately he'd heard about it before he came here. I persuaded him not to talk about it to the others.'

'No, so he did something that was much more cruel. And you kept quiet and let him get away with it.'

He looked annoyed.

'I've explained to you before, Miss Bray, that it isn't the

151

function of a psychiatrist to sit in judgement on people. My role is to help them understand why they behave in the way that they do.'

'And you hoped to make Ralph Keyson understand why he'd scared Stanley Gorton half to death?'

'Yes, if given time.'

'Was that why you kept the piece of inner tube?'

'I thought it might be helpful at some future time to confront him with an objective correlative of an otherwise deniable action.'

'In other words, yes.'

'In other words, if you like, yes.'

We stared at each other. I wondered if he understood me as little as I understood him. I'd asked to see him immediately after breakfast and had expected at least some embarrassment when I told him what I'd discovered. He'd reacted instead by being surprised again at my anger, as if it were a psychological symptom.

'So you tucked it away in your records. I suppose it fell out of the file when Mrs Minter stole them.'

'Presumably.'

'And made a note of it on Stanley Gorton's file. I notice you didn't ask Jenny Chesney to type that note, by the way. You didn't tell her about this?'

He shook his head.

'Don't you think you should have told her, in the circumstances?'

'Do you think that would have been helpful?'

'It might have helped to warn her away from a friendship with a very unpleasant man.'

'You tend to talk, Miss Bray, as if I should be some kind of moral traffic policeman. That's not my duty.'

'What is your duty? Standing by to watch the collision?'

'Sometimes, yes.'

I sighed, exasperated, and got up to go. He stopped me.

'There was something I forgot to tell you when you got back yesterday.'

'Something else, you mean.'

'The police inspector came back. Apparently they've

tested the revolver the fingerprints. They found only two sets on it, Ralph Keyson's, and Hal Hunter's.'

'What did the inspector say about that?'

'I had the impression that he thought it wrapped up the case neatly: suicide.'

'I doubt if Brigadier Moss will agree.'

I left him and walked out to the front lawn. There was piano music coming from the common room, not long sweeps of Tchaikovsky like the night before, but little runs and snatches. As I went nearer to the open French windows I recognised it as part of the accompaniment to that saddest of song cycles, Schubert's *Winterreise*. In the middle of that hot summer the piano was giving out despair and winter cold. I followed the sound inside and found that David was playing to nobody but himself. He looked up when he saw me, nodded, but went on playing. It was the song about a man listening to a street musician grinding out a monotonous little tune on a hurdy-gurdy. I'd never heard anything more bleak than the way David was playing it. It seemed to drive the sun itself out of the room and let in grey winter light. I sat down on a sofa and looked at him.

'Still detecting, Nell? It's a waste of time, you know.'

The tune made its own mocking comment.

'Why do you say that?'

'Because you're looking for something that's not there.'

'I've found something already.'

'Then it must be the wrong thing.'

The tune went on grinding out from under his fingers as he talked, as if it had nothing to do with him, as if none of this had anything to do with him.

'Have you heard about the fingerprints?'

Only the tune answered, and it didn't care.

'There are only two sets of fingerprints on that gun, Hal Hunter's, who found it, and Ralph Keyson's.'

'I know.'

He let the tune come to its end, paused a second, then set it going again.

'How did you know? Did Dr Stroud tell you?'

153

He shook his head.

'He didn't need to. I was there when they were put on the gun in the first place.'

'When?'

He smiled and let the tune mock both of us.

'Come along, Nell. Surely you've guessed that. You remember after Hal found the gun, Stroud told Hal to look after it. Then he went back to the house with you and Jacko and left Hal and me on guard with the body. It was Hal who remembered about fingerprints.'

'What did you do?'

'Wiped it clean with a handkerchief, put Keyson's paw round it, then Hal picked it up just as he'd done the first time. I'm glad the police appreciate the trouble we took.'

'I don't suppose Brigadier Moss will.'

'What could he do about it?'

'Charge you with interfering with evidence.'

'He couldn't. You know that gun has nothing to do with the evidence. It was put by that post at least half an hour after Keyson was shot. I saw you searching all along that fence. If it had been there in the first place, you'd have found it.'

'But you said you hadn't been watching me. You let everybody think I was talking nonsense.'

For a moment indignation at his disloyalty pushed out other thoughts. He laughed and put an extra trill into the hurdy-gurdy.

'When Hal or Jacko had gone to all the trouble of planting that gun there, I wasn't going to spoil it, was I?'

'You think Hal or Jack Kelso put it there?'

'Of course. Who else?'

'And you decided to keep quiet about it and arrange a set of fake fingerprints to protect Hal or Jacko?'

'Yes. Ironic – in the circumstances.'

Another trill.

'Which must mean you were convinced at the time that either Hal or Jacko had shot him. Or perhaps both of them together.'

I watched his face. It gave nothing away.

154

'That's what I thought at the time, yes.'

'But you don't think that now?'

'No.'

'Why not?'

He was playing his own variations on the tune now, taking it through windings that came back to the same doleful little melody.

'Because now, my dear Nell, I know who did it.'

I was astounded. I knew how good his mind was when he chose to use it, but had the impression he'd put it into storage for the duration of the war. I'd been wrong. I tried to keep my tone as light as his, since that seemed to be the way he wanted it.

'Really. Would you be kind enough to share your knowledge with me?'

Another variation, more complicated. I sat as patiently as I could, trying not to be annoyed with him. If he had got there before me he deserved his triumph. He brought the variation neatly back to its starting point and smiled at me as in the old days, pleased with himself.

'You really want to know who killed Ralph Keyson?'

'Yes.'

'I hope you mean it.' Trill. 'I did.'

'No!'

I found myself standing beside him, holding his right hand hard down on the piano keys, associating the mocking tune with what he'd told me, trying to stop it. He looked up at me, smile twisted now, and went on picking out the tune with his left hand.

'I thought you wanted to know.'

'I don't believe you. If it's a joke, it's not funny.'

'No, not a joke. Not more than anything else anyway. Sit down, Nell. I can't tell you if you're standing over me.'

I went back to the sofa as if the room had become an aquarium and we were both floating in it, no contact left with anything outside. David stopped playing and sat sideways on the piano stool, looking down at his hands.

'I've been having dreams, Nell.'

'Dreams!'

'Listen. Soon after he came here, I'd dream I was stabbing at somebody with a bayonet. The bayonet wouldn't come out and when I pulled it the body would come falling towards me. It always had Ralph Keyson's face.'

'But that doesn't mean . . .'

'Listen. I told Dr Stroud about it, of course, and we discussed it. At one level it was simple old wish fulfilment. Anyway, after a week or so Julius managed to get me shifted off that dream onto some others that were more interesting from our point of view and didn't have Keyson in them. Until last night – when he came back again.'

He said that quite simply, as if Keyson had merely walked in at the door. He wasn't trying to impress or be clever now, simply explaining to me.

'Brigadier Moss asked me on Friday about that argument I had with him, so I suppose that helped to bring it out. Anyway, whatever the reason, last night it all came back. It was bright moonlight, just as it was on Thursday night, and I was walking along the top of the bank with a revolver in my hand. I saw Keyson there standing by the fence, looking out over the field with his back to me. I slid down into the ditch, keeping very quiet, and crawled along it. I'd had plenty of practice at that on wire patrols. I crawled until I was level with him, then I stood up in the ditch and put a bullet through the back of his head. He never even knew I was there.'

'David, it was a dream.'

'Dreams don't come from nowhere. Anyway, the next thing I knew in my dream I was walking uphill beside the fence, still with the gun. I simply stretched my arm out and dropped it. Then I went on walking uphill feeling more free than I'd felt for years and years. That's where the dream ended.'

'Didn't you hear me shout?'

'When?'

'In your dream, I shouted.'

He shook his head.

'I can't remember. Anyway, that's beside the point. My

conscious memory starts from the time I came down the hill and saw you there beside his body. I'd no idea then, of course. I thought I'd just been out walking as usual. I'd repressed the whole thing completely until last night. I sat there beside his body and thought Hal or Jacko had done it, and good luck to them.'

'But the gun. Why should Hal or Jacko put it there to make it look like suicide if they hadn't done it?'

'Exactly the same reason as when I thought I was covering up for them. One of them must have found the gun and decided it would do better down by his body. They must have thought I was a cool customer.'

He laughed.

'Don't do that.'

'Sorry Nell. If I'd remembered this before I'd have saved everybody a lot of trouble.'

'I don't believe you.'

At last there was a hint of regret on his face, like a boy who's been clumsy and broken something.

'Don't worry about me more than you can help. Guilty but insane, I dare say. If not . . .' He shrugged.

'A dream isn't evidence.'

'Dreams are the royal road to the knowledge of the unconscious.'

'Who says so?'

'Dr Freud.'

'Damn Dr Freud and all his works. You used to have a mind. Do you seriously expect me to believe you killed a man because you dreamed it?'

'Very well, let's look at the evidence. Who was first on the scene after you got there?'

'You were, but . . .'

'Is it or is it not a fact that a gun disappeared and reappeared? Doesn't my dream explain it?'

'It doesn't explain anything.'

I heard the door open. Somebody looked in at us and walked away again. Jenny, from the sound of the steps.

'What about the grenade? Did you throw that as well, in your dream?'

157

'Sorry, nothing about grenades.'

'Have you told anybody else about this dream?'

'Dr Stroud.'

'What did he say?'

'That it was interesting.'

'He took it seriously?'

'He takes all dreams seriously.'

'And did he suggest what you should do about it?'

'What he always suggests – that I dream again tonight and we discuss it tomorrow.'

'Well, for goodness sake don't tell anybody else.'

'Why not?'

'Because if Brigadier Moss hears about it he'll jump to conclusions.'

'I might save him the trouble.'

'David, please . . .'

He closed his eyes.

'Don't ask me to start running and dodging again, Nell. I can cope with almost anything, but not that. I'm tired, simply bone tired.'

I went out. As I closed the door he started playing again, that endless, hopeless, hurdy-gurdy tune.

I wanted to kick somebody. The person I wanted to kick was Dr Sigmund Freud. Since he was unobtainable in person I went up to my room and kicked his photograph, the one that had been salvaged from Dr Stroud's study. The glass, already shattered, fell from the frame, the picture wire it had hung by curled out over the floor. I paused in my kicking. There seemed to be a great quantity of picture wire, more than would have been needed to keep it in place, several feet of it at least. Dr Freud's eyes watched me coldly from the photograph as I knelt on the floor and coiled it up. A dream isn't evidence nor, in itself, is a length of picture wire. But I'd already seen that day what an ingenious mind could do with two bamboo canes and a piece of bicycle inner tube. More kicking of Dr Freud would have to wait. The urgent thing was to have another talk with Mrs Monica Minter.

EIGHTEEN

DR CASPIAN AND THE PADRE were strolling on the lawn. I walked past them quickly, collecting curious glances, but I was in no mood to stop for explanations. Striding down the valley road, I tried over in my mind what I knew or had guessed. There never had been a shot into the conservatory. That was Ralph Keyson's cruel trick on Stanley Gorton. The mind that had produced that trick would be quite capable of working out a booby trap with a grenade, taking particular pleasure in it because a grenade was the weapon that Stanley Gorton used in trying to commit his own crime. Quite how the booby trap was to have worked I still didn't know. Possibly the grenade had been wedged upright with a piece of wood against the side of the couch, with a length of piano wire running from the wedge over the nail that had held Dr Freud's picture. If that wire ran to the outside of the window, then a strong pull on the wire would carry the wedge away.

Hal Hunter had seen Mrs Minter outside that window. Ralph Keyson had been up and about earlier that morning, watching me from the conservatory. Ralph Keyson and Mrs Minter were old family friends. They might have arranged to meet and set up the booby trap together. After that, once Keyson knew the time of Gorton's appointment, it should be a simple matter for him to stroll by the flower bed under Dr Stroud's window, tug the wire and retire to a safe distance in the few seconds before the explosion.

For some reason, perhaps the presence of other people on the lawn, he hadn't done it after all. Which would have left Ralph Keyson in a very nasty situation indeed, knowing that at midday he was due to take his place on the very couch where he'd wedged a live grenade. Robin Duncan had been saved by his own bad temper, refusing to lie down on the couch at all. So what was Keyson to do?

'Bollocks.'

I said it aloud. A censorious sheep glared at me. Somebody had scrawled the word on the orders for hospital patients just outside Dr Stroud's study. If that person had been Colonel Ralph Keyson himself sometime earlier that would have given him a very useful excuse to pause for a minute on the way into the study. In that minute, the grenade had exploded. If my guess about the working of the booby trap was right, then an accomplice must have operated it from outside the window. But who was the accomplice? Not, on this occasion, Monica Minter, because she was on her way to the meeting at Abergavenny. Keyson, in desperate need, must have found somebody else to do it.

At that point I stopped short. Suppose that theoretical accomplice had turned unreliable once he, or she, saw the effects of the explosion. Supposing there'd been an argument and that argument had ended with a bullet in the back of Ralph Keyson's head. Either that or the person had said something to Stanley Gorton and Gorton had guessed what Keyson was trying to do to him. He had, after all, tried to kill somebody with far less reason than that. I started downhill again, almost running. Brigadier Moss might be back at any time and David, in his present mood, was quite capable of going to him and confessing to murder. It was up to me to find the real murderer for the Brigadier before that happened.

By the time I was ringing the bell on the step between two curly brick pillars my straw hat was wilted, my boots and skirt covered with white dust. I had to wait for some time. It was near lunchtime and the domestic staff were probably busy in the kitchen and dining room. The air hung heavily over the garden, almost suffocating with the scent of roses. I could see a sloping section of lawn at the

160

back of the house and a gardener leading a small donkey across it, attached to a mowing machine. The donkey had probably been called into service because the household pony had been conscripted for war work. Even horses were being requisitioned for service in the Flanders mud. Given Mrs Minter's views, the diminutive donkey itself was lucky to have escaped. One of the pamphlets handed out by the Duty and Discipline Movement asked: 'Have you a man digging your garden who should be digging trenches?' This gardener looked seventy at least and bent with rheumatism. Old men, invalids and donkeys – that was what the war was leaving us. I tried not to think of David, to wonder if Brigadier Moss was on his way back to Nantgarrew.

An elderly maid opened the door and gave me a suspicious look. I said I'd like to see Mrs Minter.

'She's working at her papers.'

'Will you please tell her that Nell Bray would like to speak to her.'

I knew this would bring her. The maid gave me another old-fashioned look and closed the front door on me. It took perhaps half a minute to deliver the message. Seconds after that there were fast footsteps in the hall, almost running, and the door was flung open. Nobody could accuse Monica Minter of trying to avoid a fight. She stood there in a blue suit and white blouse of severe military cut, hair a little dishevelled, eyes a whole artillery barrage.

'Well?'

'We might start,' I said, 'by discussing why you committed a theft.'

I made no attempt to keep my voice down. The maid was standing at the end of the passage, open-mouthed. From a side room I heard the ladylike voice of Mrs Minter's aunt.

'Who is it, Monica?'

'Don't worry, aunt. I'm dealing with this.'

The way she said 'this' was intended to place me among life's nasty little incidents.

161

She shut the front door behind her and walked quickly round the side of the house. I followed. When the ancient gardener saw her coming he withdrew at a fast hobble, taking donkey and mower with him. She marched up the mown half of the lawn and stopped by a small summer house in a grove of silver birch trees.

'How dare you accuse me of theft?'

'How else would you get your hands on those records?'

'It isn't stealing to disclose treason.'

'What's your name for it then, espionage behind enemy lines?'

'You find that amusing? You'd sneer at the men and women who are risking their lives daily for King and Country?'

She'd fallen into something of her platform manner although there was no audience apart from me and the birds in the birch trees. I kept my voice at conversational pitch.

'I don't sneer at anybody who's caught up in this terrible business, but I fail to see anything heroic in filching confidential records from a doctor's study.'

'Then you haven't thought about it. There's a more dangerous enemy for this land of ours than German bombers or machine-gunners. There's the unseen enemy who does the Kaiser's filthy work in the very heart of our country like a foul maggot in a lovely English apple, eating its poisonous way to all that is dearest and best in it, hoping that collapse from the inside will undermine the defences that no assault from outside can breach.'

That made, by my count, a quadruple mixed metaphor, a new record in my fairly considerable platform experience. It was hardly the time to point that out.

'I take it you're claiming that Nantgarrew is such a threat to the war effort that any measures against it are justified.'

'I shouldn't expect you to know anything about courage, not even ordinary decent courage, let alone the sort it takes to descend to fight the rats in the sewer but stay unsoiled.'

'It's obvious at any rate that Brigadier Moss doesn't

approve of your methods.'

It was a shot in the dark, based on the argument between them in Swansea, but I saw her jaw muscles tighten and knew I'd scored a hit.

'Brigadier Moss is an imbecile.'

'I'd have thought you regarded him as one of our brave defenders. But perhaps he didn't care for the cowardly tactics in that speech of yours.'

'Cowardly!'

The way she shot the word out sent the birds scattering from the birch trees.

'It's usually considered cowardly to attack a sick man.'

'If you mean Stanley Gorton, he's no more than a common criminal.'

'How did you know his name? He was Mr Bird in that report you quoted.'

'What does it matter what his name is? He should have been shot.'

'Was that why you and your friend Ralph Keyson were trying to kill him?'

There was shock in her expression, and fear.

'Have you gone mad?'

'Do you deny that Colonel Keyson was an old friend of yours?'

'I'm not discussing Colonel Keyson with you.'

'Was it your idea or his to use a hand grenade?'

'Quite mad.'

'That was what you were doing outside Dr Stroud's window on Thursday morning, wasn't it? You were fixing up your end of the trap, probably pegging the wire down in the flower bed.'

'I don't know what you're talking about.'

'You said it was a little surprise for us all.'

'Oh, that.'

She laughed. I could sense tension falling away from her.

'Haven't you found out the answer to that yet? What a lazy lot of people you are.'

She stood there, smiling at me. I was aware I'd taken a false step and put her back on the offensive, but I couldn't

163

for the life of me see where I'd made my mistake.

'Do you deny having anything to do with the grenade explosion in Dr Stroud's study on Thursday?'

'I refuse to answer such a ridiculous question. Since you've come intruding here, there's a question I want to put to you. Not that I'll get an honest answer.'

'What is it?'

'Who shot Ralph Keyson?'

'I don't know. I'm trying to find out.'

'By asking me impertinent questions. Why aren't you asking them up at Nantgarrew?'

'Because I'm almost certain that his death is connected in some way with two cruel attacks he made on Stanley Gorton.'

'And you naturally take the side of a traitor against the memory of a brave man. Was it Gorton who killed him?'

'I don't know.'

'You'd shield the murderer, of course, whoever it was.'

'I wonder if you're doing some shielding yourself. For instance, what were you doing at Nantgarrew in the early hours of Friday morning?'

'Are you accusing me of killing him?'

It came out almost as a shriek. She was close to losing control.

'I'm not accusing anybody yet, just asking questions.'

'Well, go back and ask them where the murderers are.'

I still had one all-important question to ask her but it would have to wait until we were nearer the house. I didn't know whether she was carrying a revolver in the pocket of her skirt. If so, anything that cramped her style in using it, even the presence of the elderly aunt or rheumatic gardener, would be a help. I shrugged as if I'd given up any hope of finding out anything from her and walked away down the lawn. When we got near the corner of the house I turned to face her.

'Were you having a love affair with Colonel Keyson?'

When I saw the look in her eyes I dodged sideways and felt the wind of her hand against my cheek. She almost overbalanced onto me, recovered herself and went, fingers hooked, for my eye sockets. I caught her wrists, forcing them apart and back, trying to get her off-balance. Luckily I'd had plenty of practice against some of the more aggressive members of the Metropolitan Police on suffragette marches, but then so had she. She bit me hard on the right forearm, fetching blood through the blouse.

'Ma'am, have you finished on the lawn, ma'am?'

Goodness knows what the gardener thought we were doing. Perhaps to his blurred sight it looked like a new system of physical exercise. Perhaps, after months of Mrs Minter, he'd decided that his best course was not to notice anything. I let go of her wrists and she closed her lips over bloodstained front teeth.

'Yes, Williams. You can finish mowing it as soon as the donkey's had his lunch.'

I couldn't help admiring the speed of her recovery. Now I knew she had no weapon worse than teeth and fingernails I let her walk me round to the front of the house. When we were out of sight and hearing of the gardener she stopped and faced me.

'You besmirch everything you touch. You can't see anything fine and noble without wanting to spread your slime all over it.'

'Does that mean the answer is no?'

She took no notice. I don't think I've ever seen anybody so angry. Her shoulders, her breasts, her whole body were shaking with it.

'As for you, you're a friend of that blonde harlot and you dare to come here and ask me if I'm . . . if I'm . . .'

The words wouldn't come out, and their refusal made her anger even more violent.

'Who is the blonde harlot in question?'

'Miss Jenny Chesney.'

She said the name like a curse.

'Are you saying that because she was a friend of Colonel Keyson too?'

'Her? He wouldn't touch filth like that with the toe of his boot. Are you claiming you don't know what's going on up there? You go back and ask your little harlot friend. Go back, go back, go back.'

Her voice rose and she made shooing movements with her hands, for all the world like somebody trying to see off an intrusive goose or gander. It would almost have been funny, unless you were standing where I was and could feel the anger coming off her in waves. I turned and walked away down the drive.

The road back looked hot and dusty. I decided to escape from the stifling valley and look for some fresh air on top of the hills. I needed to clear my mind before going back to Nantgarrew. That's what I told myself, but I knew I was really putting off the conversation I must have with Jenny.

I followed a footpath up through the sheep pasture and came out on the top of the ridge. There was, as I'd hoped, a breeze up there with a smell of warm peat. A hare loped across the path and a skylark sang. But the path my mind was taking was a less attractive one. On the night Keyson died, I'd gone to Jenny's room and found her bed empty. Suppose she'd crept downstairs to meet him and Mrs Minter had found them together by the fence. I'd just had a demonstration that sexual matters had a powerful effect on Monica Minter. Might the effect have been so powerful that she'd simply taken out her trusty revolver and let fly? But if so, why had she shot her friend Keyson and not poor Jenny?

I wished the skylark would keep quiet. There was a worse possibility, that it was Monica Minter who had the secret assignation with Keyson and Jenny who'd found them. In that case, discovering Keyson's disloyalty both to herself and Nantgarrew, could it be Jenny who'd done the shooting? Mrs Minter would know, but Mrs Minter couldn't accuse Jenny without admitting her own unfaithfulness to her husband serving in the North Sea. It would account for her violent, almost insane hatred of Jenny.

I came back to the grenade, convinced that the key to the murder was there. Surely Jenny couldn't have been Keyson's accomplice. She'd been walking on the lawn with me when the grenade exploded. In any case, I couldn't get away from the fact that Mrs Minter had been doing something at Nantgarrew that morning, and I still didn't know what it was.

I walked a mile or so until I saw Nantgarrew and its silver gash of waterfall almost below me. I paused to look at it before taking the path down. I could see two men strolling down the drive in the afternoon sun, one of them the Padre by his black coat. There were two or three others sitting on the lawn. The patches of brown mange on the lawn seemed to have got worse. Odd, because you'd expect a lawn to shrivel in the heat at much the same rate, not in irregular patches. It looked like a pattern, or letters. There was something like a large 'C' near the flagpole, then a circle, then what might have been a cramped 'W'. I stood and spelt it out. 'C.O.W.' then something that might have been an 'A' or an 'N', possibly an 'R', indisputably a 'D', then a kind of scribble close up against the flower bed under Dr Stroud's window. Then it leapt out at me. Written in brown patches on Nantgarrew's lawn in letters several feet wide was the word 'COWARD', with the scribble on the end that must have been the 'S' she was making when Hal Hunter interrupted her.

Caustic soda in a watering can would have done it. I'd even tripped over the watering can. I now knew what surprise Monica Minter had been preparing at Nantgarrew in the early hours of Thursday morning, and it didn't help at all.

NINETEEN

THERE WAS SOMETHING ELSE SPOILING the view of Nantgarrew. I'd have noticed it before if I hadn't been spelling out the letters on the lawn. Standing there on the drive by the front of the house, drab against the gravel in its brown paint, was a motor vehicle. Brigadier Moss's vehicle. The uniformed driver was doing something to the engine. The men sitting on the lawn had turned their backs on it, aware it meant trouble. When I saw it I started running down the hill, skidding on the dry grass.

The first person I saw when I got back to the grounds was Jack Kelso. He was sitting on the steps by the shrubbery. He stood up when he saw me and grinned, but it was a strained attempt.

'He's back then.'

'An hour ago.'

He must have passed me while I was walking up to the ridge.

'Who's in with him?'

'Stanley Gorton. Asked for him as soon as he got here.'

He must have noticed the relief on my face.

'Makes sense, doesn't it Miss?'

'Sense?'

'He'd tried to pull a trick with a grenade once before.'

'You knew about that?'

'Of course. We all knew it. It was only Ralph Red-Tabs kept on about it.'

'And the shooting?'

'Well, if it was Stanley Gorton, I don't blame him.

Keyson was making his life a misery – hints, looks, never left him alone.'

I said: 'You didn't think it was Gorton when we found the body.'

'I wasn't thinking much either way.'

'But you did what you could to help whoever shot him. Was it you who put the gun there or Captain Hunter?'

'Wasn't it there all the time?'

A grin. Well, I couldn't expect an honest answer to that.

'Have you seen David Ellward?'

'No. He wasn't in at lunchtime.'

'Did Brigadier Moss ask about him?'

'Not that I know.'

Silence. Jacko seemed to be making up his mind to say something else.

'I hope I'm not intruding where I'm not wanted, but you wouldn't let Lieutenant Ellward do anything silly, would you Miss?'

The question sounded casual enough, but his eyes were fixed on my face.

'Like what, Jack?'

'Sometimes he talks a bit wildly. It doesn't mean anything, but Brigadier Moss wouldn't know that.'

'What about Jenny? He wanted to talk to her the other day, didn't he?'

'Yes. He'll be back to her. He'll be back to all of us unless he gets what he wants.'

I thought what Jack must be thinking. Let him fix on Gorton. Let him carry fat, devious Gorton away with him down the valley, do with him what he liked and leave the rest of us alone. It could so easily have been Stanley Gorton.

'There were two of your grenades stolen, weren't there?'

'Yes.'

'We know what became of one. I wonder what happened to the other.'

'He'd need one in reserve, wouldn't he?'

'Who?'

'Whoever it was threw it.'

169

'If it was thrown.'

I decided to take a chance and told him about my theory of the booby trap. I could tell by the way he listened that he was weighing it up as a technical problem.

'Well, could it be done?'

'That depends. You'd need a strong wedge keeping it upright. There's a powerful spring on those levers. Then you'd need a good tug on the wedge when you wanted it to topple over and go off.'

'Could you do it through the window?'

'If you got it fixed up that way, yes. Is that how it happened?'

'I think so.'

'Still, it doesn't help us much, does it? Whoever shot him did it the old-fashioned way, and that's what the Brigadier's interested in.'

'We stood in silence, looking down at the house. Jack sighed.

'It's the finish of all this, anyway.'

'Of Nantgarrew?'

'Yes. They don't like colonels getting killed.'

'What will happen to you all?'

'Oh, I suppose they'll send us back, all except the worst ones and they'll find somewhere else for them.'

'To the trenches?'

'Yes. About time I went back anyway.'

He sounded as casual as a man about to go out and do a bit of gardening. You wouldn't have guessed he still had nightmares about Germans and shell holes.

'Surely you don't want to go. This war must be over soon. If you could only stay out of it for another two or three months . . .'

'I've got some good friends out there. Had some, anyway.'

I left him sitting on the steps, staring at nothing.

The house was dark and quiet, apart from a murmur of voices from the common room. The door to Dr Stroud's study was firmly shut. I looked into Jenny's office, found it deserted and went upstairs. As I opened the door of my room there was a movement inside and there was Jenny half-way out of a chair, eyes wide with strain and tiredness, skin stretched over her cheekbones, tight as the hide on a drum. Tendrils of hair round her face were damp as if she'd been sponging it with an unsteady hand. Her look as I came in was blank fear.

'Nell, where have you been?'

'Talking to Mrs Minter again. Did you know Ralph Keyson was an old friend of hers?'

She shook her head. The fear hadn't gone from her face even when she'd seen it was me.

'Are you sure? He never mentioned it to you?'

'Never.'

She seemed to find it hard to speak.

'I'm afraid there are some other things you didn't know about him.'

I pressed her shoulder to make her sit down again in the chair. Her bones felt sharp under my hand.

'He'd come here to spy on Nantgarrew. I don't know if the War Office sent him or if he and Mrs Minter worked it out together. Either way, he must have believed this nonsense about undermining the war effort.'

Her knuckles were pressed against her teeth.

'Hadn't you suspected?'

She shook her head.

'Perhaps it seemed like a useful way to spend his convalescence. He must have known enough about psychoanalysis to fake some convincing symptoms.'

'How do you know this?'

'It's the only thing that make sense. If he was feeding information back, that would explain how Brigadier Moss is so well informed about what happens here. I suspect he was working for the War Office and helping his old friend Mrs Minter as a sideline. I don't think Brigadier Moss was very pleased when he found out about that.'

She moved her head from side to side, as if she couldn't take in what I was telling her.

'I've been so stupid Nell, so stupid.'

'For not guessing? Why should you?'

'More than that.'

I waited for her to go on. She didn't.

'There's no shame in being in love with somebody.'

'Of course not. We've all read our Ibsen and our H.G. Wells, haven't we?'

'Don't blame yourself. Naturally you admired him at first.'

'Oh yes. Dr Freud would have said I was looking for a father figure.'

Colonel Keyson, I supposed, had been about ten years older than Jenny. Were women supposed to want to murder their fathers too, according to Dr Freud, or was that just men? I could hardly ask Jenny.

'You'd guessed from the start, hadn't you, Nell?'

'I sensed there was some reason for bringing me here, apart from what you wrote in your letter. Then the day after I arrived, when he apparently just missed being blown up by a grenade . . .'

'Don't.'

'The ironic thing was, you wrote that letter because you were worried about what happened in the conservatory. But he was in no danger when that happened, no danger at all.'

'What do you mean?'

I told her what I'd discovered about the trick Keyson had played on Stanley Gorton. Her face was frozen, the expression unreadable.

'Dr Stroud knew about this. He guessed as soon as it happened.'

She whispered: 'He didn't tell me.'

'No. I think that was wrong of him. It was dangerous too because Ralph Keyson went on to plan something worse.'

I've been accused, by Jenny among others, of tactlessness. If there is a tactful way to tell a woman that her lover tried to murder somebody I hope I find it before the next time. As it was I told it as baldly as I could, what I knew and what I'd guessed. When I got to the point where the two men were standing just outside the door while the grenade went off inside she shivered and put her head in her hands.

'You didn't know anything about this, Jenny? Didn't guess anything?'

'No.'

Her voice came muffled.

'Jenny, I'm sorry. I know you . . .'

She sat up suddenly.

'I'm glad he's dead, Nell. After what you tell me, he deserves to be dead.'

Her voice was hard, her eyes quite dry.

'Don't talk like that.'

'Why not?'

'Because if Brigadier Moss heard you he might think . . .'

'That I killed him myself.'

'Yes. I'm afraid he already knows about the two of you.'

'Why?'

'Because Monica Minter knows.'

'About us two? That woman?'

'I'm afraid so.'

'What exactly did she say, Nell? In her own words.'

'She called you a blonde harlot.'

She laughed, an odd, cold giggle.

'How very Biblical of her. There were always people shouting that at us on suffragette marches, weren't there? Do you remember that clergyman with the umbrella in Trafalgar Square?'

'Vividly, but that's not the point now. She obviously said it because she's eaten up with jealousy of you.'

'Monica Minter jealous? Of me? Why?'

She seemed genuinely incredulous. It wasn't surprising if her brain wasn't at its best, after all the shocks I'd had to give her.

'I'd have thought that was obvious. I told you Ralph Keyson was an old friend of hers. I think it probably went a lot further than that.'

'You mean they were . . . lovers.'

She seemed to find it hard to believe and I sympathised. I wondered which would be worse, to know that your lover had attempted murder or that he'd been unfaithful with somebody you despised.

173

'Whether they did the deed, I don't know. But I'm sure there was an attraction there. She tried to claw my eyes out when I asked her about it.'

Another cold giggle.

'I'm not surprised. You always did plunge in, Nell. Don't say anything for a moment. Let me think.'

She sat staring out of the window. I could feel her building up barriers against me. I didn't blame her. She could hardly take all this from me and stay friends. It was several minutes before she said anything, then her voice was calm.

'So you had the impression that Mrs Minter was in love with Ralph Keyson and is jealous of me. I take it the reason for that is you think she knows Ralph Keyson and myself were lovers.'

'Yes.'

'And that she's passed that little fact on to Brigadier Moss?'

'Probably, yes.'

'Well then, I'm in trouble, aren't I? Like poor Gwenda.'

'You're not . . .?'

'Oh no, not that sort of trouble. But you know how he behaves to erring womankind.'

'Yes. I think you'll have a bad time with him. For instance, he'll ask you where you were and what you were doing the night Ralph Keyson was killed.'

'Yes.'

'You must tell him the truth about meeting Robin. He's on his way to the Baltic by now. It can't do him any harm. Brigadier Moss won't be pleased. He might even threaten to prosecute you for aiding a deserter, but it's safer than lying to him.'

'Yes.'

'In fact, there is one lie that won't hurt. You can tell him that you jumped out in front of Robin and tried to stop him but couldn't. It's near enough. You needn't tell him you thought Robin was somebody else.'

'No.'

'But Jenny, just for my own curiosity, who did you expect

to see coming down the road?'

'Ralph Keyson.'

She almost whispered the two words.

'He was dead by then, Jenny.'

'I didn't know that. I'd gone to his room and he wasn't there. I went out looking for him. I couldn't find him in the house or garden, so I went down the drive. That was when I saw Mrs Minter.'

'You really did see her?'

'Yes.'

'Then you'll have to tell Brigadier Moss that as well.'

'Yes. I suppose he will be coming back. When do you think, Nell? Tomorrow?'

'He's here already.'

She jumped up and gave a little scream, cut off abruptly.

'Here? Why didn't you tell me?'

'What difference does it make, today or tomorrow?'

'All the difference in the world, Nell. Let me go.'

She dodged round me and was out of the door, slamming it behind her. I heard her running downstairs. What was it that I still didn't know about Jenny?

TWENTY

I FOLLOWED HER MORE SLOWLY, but by the time I got down to the hall she'd disappeared. Instead there was Stanley Gorton standing in a pool of shadow like a night creature that had seen too much of the daylight. I thought he looked guilty when he saw me, but he tried to smile.

'Ah, Miss Bray. Come for your session with Brigadier Moss?'

'Not that I know of. You were with him a long time.'

He gave me another twitch of a smile.

'There were ... er ... a few things he thought I could help him with.'

'What sort of things?'

Before he could answer we heard Brigadier Moss's voice. It came from the other side of the door in Jenny's office.

'What do you think you're doing, Miss Chesney?'

I heard the murmur of Jenny's voice, but couldn't make out what she said. Stanley Gorton's plump tongue flickered over his lips. Then Brigadier Moss again, even louder.

'Well, you've got no business to do it. You should have asked my permission before coming in here.'

I wondered whether to intervene when the door of Dr Caspian's room on the other side of the hall was flung open and Dr Stroud strode out. He crossed the hall in two strides, looking furious, and pushed open the door of Jenny's office.

'What's going on?'

I edged nearer so that I could see into the room. Jenny,

176

face flushed, was standing by her desk, Brigadier Moss glaring at her. He turned round and transferred the glare to Dr Stroud.

'You will kindly explain to your assistant that she has no right to come in here without authorisation.'

He put stress on the words 'your assistant', apparently implying that the doctor was failing to control his staff. Stroud was visibly trying to restrain his anger.

'It is Miss Chesney's office, after all.'

'It's been requisitioned.'

He might as well have said conquered and occupied. Jenny, standing her ground, looked at Dr Stroud.

'I needed some of the records.'

Her eyes pleaded with him to support her. He said to Brigadier Moss:

'That's hardly unreasonable, is it? We are a working hospital after all.'

'Are you, Major Stroud? I've seen very few signs of it so far. The records are requisitioned too. Everything in these rooms is requisitioned until further notice.'

Jenny opened her mouth to protest. Dr Stroud said hastily:

'Miss Chesney, would you please find Dr Caspian and tell him I shall have to go on using his office.'

The look she gave him showed she knew he was finding an excuse to send her away before she said something unforgivable to Brigadier Moss. She refused to be hurried, opened her desk drawer and took something out while the two men stared at her.

'What's that?'

Moss rapped out the question. She showed him a notebook.

'What's that you've got underneath it?'

For a moment it looked as if she was going to defy him, then she lifted up the notebook and revealed a small key.

'Give it to me, please, Miss Chesney.'

'It's to my private drawer.'

'Give it to me.'

I recognised it as she handed it over. I'd last seen it in the lock of the filing cabinet by Dr Stroud's desk. She put it into Brigadier Moss's hand as if she wished it were red hot, turned and went out.

Moss pocketed the key.

'I shall be speaking to you again later, Major Stroud. Meanwhile I shall be obliged if you'll send Lieutenant Ellward to me.'

There was a movement behind me. It was Stanley Gorton, making for the front door.

'Lieutenant Ellward. Is there any particular reason . . .?'

'When I give an order I don't expect to have to give reasons.'

'I'm concerned with the welfare of my patients.'

'Are you refusing to obey an order?'

For a wild moment I thought Stroud was refusing, but surrender was inevitable. He was only trying to cover it with some rags of professional decency.

'It's not a case of . . .'

'Answer yes or no. And say "Sir" when you talk to me.'

Stroud sighed.

'No, Sir. I'm not refusing.'

'Then send Lieutenant Ellward to me. Or is there some difficulty about that?'

'It may take a little time to find him . . . Sir.'

Veins throbbed under Brigadier Moss's parchment skin.

'Are you trying to tell me that we have yet another deserter?'

'Not deserter, no. He tends to go walking in the hills. I've encouraged it as a necessary part of his treatment.'

'Ye gods.'

Brigadier Moss closed his eyes and rocked his head from side to side.

'You will find Lieutenant Ellward and send him to me within half an hour. Otherwise you will find yourself on a charge of disobeying orders and inciting desertion. Is that clear, Major Stroud?'

'Perfectly clear, Sir.'

At least, since he wasn't wearing uniform, Dr Stroud was spared the necessity of saluting. When he turned and walked out he managed, in spite of his anger, to do it in his normal civilian saunter. I could see from Brigadier Moss's expression that he was trying to work out a way of adding that to the charge sheet.

I followed Dr Stroud out of the front door and onto the lawn.

I said: 'Do you know why he wants to speak to David?'

'I assume it's because of something Stanley Gorton told him.'

'You know what will happen if he questions David? In his present mood he'll sit there and tell him that he shot Keyson, because of that damned dream.'

'Yes.'

'Couldn't you talk to Moss first, explain about the dream and make him see that it doesn't mean anything?'

'Do you think he'd listen to me if I did?'

I thought of the look on the Brigadier's face.

'Probably not.'

'Anything I could say would only make things worse.'

'It's almost as if David wants to believe he killed him.'

'Yes, I think he does. It may be a necessary process of objectifying the anger he's been trying to repress.'

'But if Moss believes him, he'll get himself shot.'

'Perhaps that's what David wants as well.'

'He's not getting it. Not if I have anything to do with it.'

'What do you propose to do?'

'We've got to stop David talking to him.'

'You heard what he said.'

'Well, at least delay finding him as long as you can. Give me time.'

'Time for what?'

'Time to convince Brigadier Moss it wasn't David.'

'I'll try, but . . .'

All the energy seemed to have drained out of him. I thought he was facing the fact that what had happened meant the end of Nantgarrew.

'I'm sorry about all this, Dr Stroud, but you know you haven't made things any easier.'

'In what way?'

'For a start, don't you think you might have told me the truth about what happened in the conservatory?'

'Oh, that.'

'Yes, ironic wasn't it? It was the shooting at the conservatory that made Jenny bring me here in the first place. I can see why you didn't tell her it was all a trick, but you might have told me.'

'I had no right . . .'

'All right, professional confidence again. But you might have hinted. You knew Ralph Keyson was an unpleasant piece of work.'

'Yes.'

'Did you ever let him know you'd found out about the trick?'

'Not directly. We discussed his attitude to Stanley Gorton.'

'Which was?'

'He had a very strongly held belief in retribution – or justice, as he preferred to call it. It may sometimes be a form of self-hatred. We want to punish other people for the unacceptable things we repress in ourselves.'

'Did his belief in retribution extend to trying to kill Stanley Gorton with a grenade?'

He bowed his head. I persisted.

'You must have thought of that.'

'Naturally, I wondered. But I don't see how he could have had anything to do with that. He was standing with me outside the door when it was thrown in through the window. Anyway, Stanley Gorton had gone by then.'

'Yes, if it had come in through the window. I don't think it did.'

I explained to him my idea about the booby trap.

'Do you remember, you announced at breakfast what patients you'd be seeing that morning? Was that the usual order?'

'Yes.'

'So he'd have known that the first person on the couch would be Stanley Gorton. If he'd set up the trap in advance it would simply be a case of standing outside and pulling on the wire. For some reason he didn't do that. So he had to detonate that grenade before his turn on the couch later in case it went off by accident.'

'But he was with me. A minute later and he'd have been on the couch.'

'Yes, but you paused at the door, didn't you. Which of you first noticed that somebody had written "Bollocks" over the regulations?'

'He did. It was the sort of thing he would notice.'

'Especially if he'd slipped into the hall earlier and written it himself.'

He was silent, staring at a brown patch of grass by our feet. I wondered whether to tell him it was part of "Cowards" but decided he had enough problems.

'Do you intend to tell Brigadier Moss about this, Miss Bray?'

'I don't know. All it proves so far is that Colonel Ralph Keyson was an unpleasant and devious man. The question is whether it has anything to do with who killed him.'

'If you're right about the grenade and Stanley Gorton had somehow guessed . . .'

'But there's no evidence that he did, is there? Wouldn't he have told you?'

'I think so.'

He glanced down the lawn. There was Gorton on the seat by the sundial, watching us, but out of earshot.

I said: 'He's been in a very nervous state. Of course, when he was planning that murder of the man in the trenches he felt a sense of calm, didn't he?'

'Sense of calm?'

'Don't you remember? It was there in the notes you made about him, the ones Mrs Minter stole.'

'Yes. I'd forgotten.'

'I think she may have had some inside help from Ralph Keyson in knowing what to steal. Did you know they were old friends?'

'No.'

He was staring at the ground again. I supposed it must be humiliating to have spent hours probing a man's mind with the latest psychoanalytical techniques and to know so little about him in the end.

'Did you know Jenny Chesney was attracted to him?'

He looked at me, weighing up whether he should say anything. In the end he just nodded his head.

'So shouldn't you have warned her, when you knew about the conservatory trick?'

'Yes, with hindsight perhaps I should.'

'At the very least, the relationship was unprofessional.'

'Yes.'

'And I'm almost sure that Brigadier Moss knows about it.'

'About Ralph Keyson and Jenny?'

'Yes.'

'That's bad.'

'Very bad. I think she should go away.'

'Another deserter?'

'At least she's not in the army.'

'I can't risk sending her away myself. You must arrange it with her. Don't tell me anything about it.'

I promised.

'And Miss Bray, you know I have to look for David. I'll delay it as long as I can, but I can't disobey a direct order.'

I told him I understood that and he went over to talk to the gardening boy who was raking the gravel. I saw him pointing down the hill, and the boy propping his rake against the wheelbarrow and putting on his jacket. If that was what the hunt for David amounted to, at least he was keeping his promise to delay things.

I walked down the lawn to where Stanley Gorton was sitting. When he saw me coming he looked alarmed and would probably have tried to escape if it hadn't been for his injured leg. Cornered as he was, he gave me another of his nervous smiles.

'Good afternoon, dear lady. Have you come to enjoy the view?'

'I've come to ask you what you've been telling Brigadier Moss about David Ellward.'

'Oh, I'm not sure we should discuss that.'

'I'm quite sure we should. What did you say to him?'

He looked round for help, found none.

'Only what he'd told me himself. I mean, he didn't make a secret of it.'

'Of what?'

'Shooting Ralph Keyson.'

'David told you he shot Ralph Keyson? When?'

'This morning. I'd gone into the common room to look for something and there he was playing this dreary little tune on the piano. So I said what about playing something more cheerful. He said all right and started playing something in ragtime.'

'At least that was more cheerful.'

'Well, yes, only it was the Dead March. He said it was for Colonel Keyson. Then he said, quite calmly, "I shot him, you know," just like that, while he was playing.'

My heart sank. It sounded all too likely.

'He was obviously joking.'

'That's what I thought at first. I told him it was in very poor taste. But then he told me exactly how he'd done it, creeping up behind him in the ditch and shooting him through the back of the head.'

He made a face as if tasting something sour.

'And you told Brigadier Moss all this?'

'What else could I do, dear lady?'

There was a smear of butter on his tie, an oily shine round his lips.

'What else could you do.'

If he noticed the dislike, he gave no sign of it. All that showed in his eyes was relief as I got up to walk away.

TWENTY-ONE

ON MY WAY BACK TO the house I had to stop to let a small procession go past. It consisted of the corporal who acted as driver for Brigadier Moss, followed by Hal Hunter and Jack Kelso. The corporal and Hunter stared straight ahead, but Jack gave me a rueful look, as if to say that what was happening had nothing to do with him. I followed them into the hall, watched as they turned right into Dr Stroud's study, then waited. It was in my mind that Brigadier Moss was organising his own search party for David, so it was something of a relief when the corporal and Jack reappeared with armfuls of files. Hal Hunter held the door open for them and the voice of Brigadier Moss from inside the study shouted to them to be careful with the damned things and not drop them. I fell in behind and watched as they carried them to the car and stowed them onto the back seat. Then all three marched back inside again. If they'd been ordered to empty the filing cabinets in Dr Stroud's study and Jenny's it would take half a dozen journeys or more.

I waited by the car while two more loads were carried out and though Hal Hunter glared at me he could hardly order me to go away. After they'd disappeared inside for the fourth time, Jenny came running to me across the lawn, shouting a question as she came.

'What are they doing Nell? What's happening?'

She came to a halt beside me, out of breath.

'It seems that Brigadier Moss has decided to commandeer all your files.'

She looked at the armfuls of them in the car and gasped.

184

Then, before I could do anything, she was burrowing in the back seat, hurling files all over the place.

'Jenny, for goodness sake, you'll only make things worse.'

She took no notice. She threw most of the files back onto the seat or the floor of the car. A few of them she grabbed and held under her arm until there was such a wad of them that she had to work one-handed. She hissed at me;:

'Nell, come and take these.'

I took them. At that point the trio reappeared and I hastily held them behind my back. When Hal Hunter saw what Jenny was doing he shouted and came running.

'The Brigadier's orders. Leave them alone.'

He snatched a file out of Jenny's hand so roughly that the cover tore. Jack made a move as if he wanted to protect Jenny, then remembered himself and stopped. The driver stared impassively.

Jenny said: 'You've no right to take those. They're medical records.'

She hadn't retreated an inch and there was hardly a tremor in her voice, although Hunter looked angry enough to hit her.

'They're army property. Brigadier Moss has decided to take them away with him.'

'Does Dr Stroud know about this?'

'It's not up to Dr Stroud.'

'I forbid you to move them. Take them out of the car at once.'

It was brave, but unwise. Hal Hunter didn't like women very much, let alone women giving him orders in front of other ranks. His face went red with anger and he swallowed several times before he managed to spit out a reply.

'Who do you think you are, woman? Do you think being an officer's whore gives you some special authority?'

That was too much for Jack Kelso, discipline or not. He stepped forward, arms full of files.

'Don't say that to her, Sir. She hasn't deserved that.'

'You keep quiet, Sergeant Kelso.'

Jack's face crumpled with hurt. If I'd been in his place I'd have been wishing that Hal Hunter had died in that shell hole. I wished it anyway. Hunter turned to the driver.

'Corporal, you will stay on guard here and make sure that neither of these women come near the vehicle.'

He jerked his head at Jack Kelso and marched back inside the house without looking at Jenny. Miserably, Jack piled his files with the others in the car.

'I'm sorry, Miss Chesney, he shouldn't have said that.'

'It's not your fault, Jack.'

But she was staring away from us down the drive.

Jack came over to where I was standing.

'Will she be all right?'

'Goodness knows.'

'It's not like him, saying a thing like that. Only he had a hard time . . .'

I was in no mood to listen to excuses for Hunter, even from Jack.

'So he's making sure everybody else has a hard time? As if it wasn't bad enough for her anyway. Ralph Keyson might not have been much of a man, but she had a right to love him if she wanted to.'

'Colonel Keyson?' Jack was staring at me, worried. 'She didn't love Colonel Keyson. He gave her the cold shivers. She told me once. She could hardly bring herself to be civil to him.'

'But . . . ' It was my turn to stare. Jack and I looked at each other across a gulf, then as in an earthquake the two sides of the gulf jumped together and I understood what he was telling me.

'So when Captain Hunter accused her of being an officer's whore . . .?'

'You must have known who he meant, Miss. We all knew, not that we'd have called her that.'

'Yes. Yes, I see.'

I was seeing more than I wanted to. The earthquake was still going on, rearranging the landscape, juggling everything I thought I'd understood.

'I'll have to go, Miss. He'll be looking for me. You'll be all right with her?'

He looked across at Jenny, still standing by the car.

'Yes. I'll take care of her. You go.'

As soon as Jack had gone into the house Jenny was at my side.

'Give them to me, Nell.'

Until then, I'd forgotten I was holding the files behind my back. Impatient, she dragged at my arm.

'I'll take them.'

'Jenny, what he said . . .'

'It doesn't matter what he said. Just give me the files.'

'What are you going to do with them?'

'Burn them. Nell, please . . .'

'Where?'

'Round the side, the kitchen garden. Give them to me. They'll be back in a minute.'

'I'll bring them.'

Short of trying to wrest them away from me there was nothing she could do about it. She led the way at a run across the drive and I followed at a fast walk, trying to hold the files so that the corporal on guard by the car didn't notice them. A path ran past the bicycle shed to a neglected patch of ground. It might have been a kitchen garden in more leisurely days. Now it consisted of two rows of lettuce run to seed, disorderly sprawls of herbs and a smouldering heap of hedge clippings and couch grass. There was no sign of the gardening boy. Jenny ran to the fire and tried to kick it into more activity.

'Bring them over here, Nell.'

There were six files, quite thick ones. I flipped the top one open and found pages of neat typescript. Part of Dr Stroud's book by the look of it.

'You don't need to read them. Bring them here.'

She'd managed to rouse the heap to a thin flame. I opened another one and saw pages I recognised.

'Nell, quickly.'

There was anger and appeal in her voice. I walked over to her.

'You haven't got time for this, Jenny. You must go away.'

187

She said nothing. The air between us wavered in the heat from the fire.

'We're very near the end of this.'

'If you'll only let me . . .'

'You're in no state to be questioned by Brigadier Moss. He's been talking to Monica Minter. Anything she may have suspected about you, she'll have passed on to him.'

She gave a little shudder.

'At the moment he thinks it was David, but that's nonsense and he'll know it before long. He's not a complete fool. You must go now, while you can.'

'But the files . . .'

'I'll see to those. I'm still on your side as far as I can be, in spite of the lies.'

'I never deliberately lied to you.'

'You let me believe a lie. It won't be so easy with Brigadier Moss.'

'I can't run away.'

'You can't stay. He might come looking for you at any moment.'

That was an exaggeration because, as far as I knew, Brigadier Moss was still occupied with the search for David. Still, it seemed to work. She wavered, looking from the fire to my face, then the files in my hands.

'Where can I go? How can I go?'

I remembered, with annoyance, that Nantgarrew was deprived of both its bicycles.

'You'll have to walk as far as Gwenda's house. Don't tell her what's happened. Just say you have to be at Abergavenny tomorrow morning. Her father will take you in the cart. Then you must take the first train to London. Have you any money with you?'

She shook her head. I found some notes in my bag and gave them to her. I had to close her fingers over them, along with the key to my house and a card with my address.

'Take a cab there. When the girl comes to clean and feed the cats, tell her you're a friend of mine. She's used to people staying.'

She was too. At various times my house has sheltered suffragists and leading members of the No Conscription Fellowship wanted for questioning by the police.

'She'll buy food for you. Don't go out unless you have to, and don't answer the door unless you hear three knocks spaced like this.' I demonstrated with my fist on the back of the files. 'That will be me.'

'When?'

'I don't know. Not more than a day, I hope.'

'What are you going to do?'

'I'll tell you when I've done it.'

'I can't go.'

'You must. If there's to be any hope at all, you must.'

'The files . . . '

I opened the thickest one, the one with the book typescript. I threw a thick handful of pages onto the fire, treading them down. The edges crisped brown but the flames were reluctant to spread.

'It will take time to burn them on this fire, more time than you've got. You must go.'

A tongue of flame licked at a couple of pages. She put the money and key in her pocket.

'That's right. Not down the drive. Over the wall there and across the fields to the road.'

She moved awkwardly, either because her ankle was still hurting her or because she was reluctant to turn her back on the fire. I helped her over the wall.

'Just keep going. I'll delay things as long as I can, until dark at any rate. Keep close to the wall then nobody will see you from the house.'

'Nell . . .'

'Off you go.'

I gave her a gentle push. I could feel the muscles of her back trembling under my hand. She began to walk, slowly at first, then faster. When I'd seen her well on the way down the field I went back to the files, put the pages I needed into my bag and stowed the rest inside the shed on my way back to the drive. It was just as well because I'd hardly set foot on the gravel before the driver pounced on

TWENTY-TWO

'YOU REALISE, MISS BRAY, THAT it's a serious offence to help a criminal to escape?'

He'd sat there behind the desk, watching as I crossed the room towards him. I suppose the effect was intended to be intimidating but it reminded me of a boys' prep school. I took my time settling into one of the grenade-scarred armchairs. At first I thought he meant Jenny, then I reminded myself that he must be thinking about one of my other offences.

'I'm not aware that I've done any such thing.'

Had he somehow found out about my last meeting with Robin Duncan?

'You don't deny that Lieutenant Ellward is an associate of yours?'

'He used to be a good friend of mine.'

'If you have any knowledge of his whereabouts, it's your duty to tell me.'

'I've no such knowledge. I assume he's gone for a walk on the hills.'

'Did he hold any conversation with you before he went?'

I let myself be angry.

'I hardly see what that has to do with you.'

'It has a great deal to do with me. Lieutenant Ellward is wanted for questioning in connection with a killing.'

'You virtually accused me of helping a criminal to escape. Did you mean David Ellward?'

'You know I did.'

'Then that implies he's a criminal. What's your proof?'

'I'm the one who's asking the questions, Miss Bray.'

'And I'm the one who's not in the army. I suppose your information comes from Stanley Gorton.'

'I refuse to discuss it.'

'Because Stanley Gorton has just come to me with some wild tale about David Ellward claiming he shot Colonel Keyson. It's a joke, a joke in very bad taste, but then David's like that. Only an imbecile like Stanley Gorton would take it seriously.'

Or another imbecile like Brigadier Moss was the implication. He didn't miss it. His jaw jutted forward like a demonstration skull at a dental school, stretching his tight skin till I expected it to tear.

'You will kindly refrain from insulting officers in my presence.'

'In your presence, Brigadier Moss, that's asking a lot.'

Part of my mind was with Jenny, wondering if she'd got as far as the road, if she'd have the sense to do as I'd told her. The more time Brigadier Moss wasted with me, the better chance she'd have to get clear. He was looking at me like a classics master faced with a defective gerund.

'You're claiming that you don't know where Lieutenant Ellward is?'

'I've told you, I don't know.'

'And you had no part in his escape?'

'It's nonsense to talk about an escape. He's just gone for a walk and he didn't consult me about it.'

He wrote something down, all part of the technique, then glanced up at me.

'That's all, Miss Bray.'

I stayed where I was. Another impatient jerk of the head.

'You can go.'

I settled deeper into the chair.

'Not yet. There are a few questions I'd like to ask you.'

'I'm too busy to hold a debate with you.'

'It won't take long. For a start, did you tell Colonel Keyson to spy on Nantgarrew or was it his own idea?'

He drew himself upright in the chair until he nearly fell over backwards.

'You are slandering the memory of a gallant officer.'

'It's possible that it was his own idea. Is it a fact that he was sent home for an operation on an ulcer and needed to convalesce?'

'Of course it is.'

'Two things could have happened after that. The first is that the War Office decided to make use of his convalescence to investigate rumours that Nantgarrew was some sort of enemy outpost. Ridiculous rumours, in any case, but just the kind of thing some people at the War Office might believe.'

'Will you please get out of my office.'

The jaw had practically dislocated itself, but he was in a dilemma and I knew it. If he'd called the corporal to throw me out, that would be an admission that he'd ordered me to go and it hadn't worked. Bad for discipline among the lower ranks.

'The second thing is that Colonel Keyson might have believed the rumours and faked nightmares to get himself sent here on his own initiative. Did you know he was an old friend of Monica Minter?'

'I don't think that's any business of yours or mine.'

'You thought it was your business in Swansea last Saturday, when you were having your argument with Mrs Minter.'

'Were you spying on me?'

'Not at all. I was spying on Monica Minter.'

His mouth fell open.

'I assume that was because you resent her patriotic activities.'

'No. It was because I was trying to find out if she'd murdered Colonel Keyson.'

'If she'd . . . you claimed they were friends.'

'I didn't know that till after her rally in Swansea. All I knew up to then was that she had a gun and a grudge against Nantgarrew. I think you were as surprised as anybody else when she produced that medical report at the meeting. Did you ask her how she got it?'

'I refuse to discuss it with you.'

'You must have realised she'd had help from somebody inside Nantgarrew. If Colonel Keyson was here as your spy and he'd been passing information to her without telling you, that would explain why you were so angry.'

'I've told you, your suspicions are both ludicrous and slanderous. In any case, I can't see why you think they have anything to do with Colonel Keyson's death.'

'Because he didn't stop at helping Mrs Minter. He was carrying on a few other little campaigns here. One of them was to terrify, even to kill, Stanley Gorton because he resented what Gorton had done in the trenches.'

'That's a ridiculous and unsupported allegation.'

But I noticed he wasn't ordering me to go any more. He kept his eyes on me, hardly blinking, while I told him about the faking of the shot into the conservatory. I even offered to take him there and demonstrate.

'Even if this farrago were true, I ask you again why you think it has anything to do with the death of Colonel Keyson.'

'Two things. The first is that it shows what kind of man Colonel Keyson was – a cruel, ingenious man who enjoyed exerting power over people. The second is that it led, a few days later, to the grenade explosion in this room. Do you expect me to believe that had nothing to do with his shooting?'

'You're accusing the late Colonel Keyson of trying to kill Lieutenant Gorton with a hand grenade?'

'I'm inviting you to work it out yourself.'

For perhaps thirty seconds I thought he might be doing exactly that. He sat there, jaw propped on his knuckles, staring at me without blinking. In spite of what I'd said to him I knew the man wasn't a fool. He might get there. Then he smiled, a smile frosty enough to crumple dahlias.

'I should at least congratulate you on your ingenuity.'

But my heart went cold, knowing that wasn't what he meant.

'Ingenuity in trying to distract me. You calculated that if you started enough false hares it would improve your friend's chances of escape.'

David or Jenny? I stared back at him, willing my face not to give anything away.

'I've told you, Lieutenant Ellward isn't escaping.'

'So you tell me. And yet you've just taken up some of my time that could have been better spent looking for him.'

Good, at least not Jenny, who was in so much greater danger than David.

'If you think that was my motive, I can honestly tell you that you're mistaken.'

'Was that all, Miss Bray?'

'There's one particular answer I'd like. Was Colonel Keyson your spy or Mrs Minter's?'

'Will you please get out of my office.'

It was more of a groan than anything. I went. It was, after all, only my curiosity because it didn't make much difference.

I made myself walk slowly out of the room, conscious of his eyes on my back. The air in the hall felt thick with the heat of a long day. There was a subdued murmur of voices from the dining room, where a cold supper had been left out to give the kitchen staff their evening free. I was sure David wouldn't be there and couldn't face questions about Jenny, so I went upstairs to my room. I had all my answers now, or all the answers I needed. The question was what I should do about them.

I shut the door behind me and watched the sunlight falling on the patchwork quilt over the bed. The quilt had a new square on its pattern, white against the bright colours. A note. I hadn't noticed it before, too preoccupied with the coming interview with Brigadier Moss. I took it in my hand. No name, nothing on the outside, just a sheet of paper from a note-book folded over. I opened it and recognised David's untidy handwriting. There were no more than a few sprawling phrases without capitals or punctuation apart from dashes, all control or order abandoned.

' – taking waistcoat and tie off – feeling of release knowing never going to be putting them on again – like fine morning in mountains but no need to plan route down – able to fly – no sense of guilt—'

I sat down on the bed.

'You utter fool.'

He'd been concerned enough about me to leave this terrible, bleak note, trusting me to understand it, but not concerned enough to talk to me. If only he had I could have given him what I didn't possess when we'd last talked over the piano, the certainty of who killed Ralph Keyson. As it was he'd gone to jump off somewhere with this for a goodbye.

The moment I read it I guessed that was what he meant. He'd always loved rock climbing. We'd spent a holiday in the Alps together just after I'd finished at Oxford. He was going to have one last climb then, from the top of it, jump down. Later I'd feel grief. Now all I could feel was anger at David himself, at the war that had caused all this, above all at the killer of Ralph Keyson. I don't know how long I sat there, numb and angry, but I hope it was no more than a minute or two because it was wasted time. When I started to think again I decided I must go out and look for his body. Somewhere with rocky crags. But the hills round us were green and rounded. There was the waterfall, but the sides of it were thickly wooded, no good for the sort of climbing David had loved. The only place I knew of locally with climbable rock faces was the old quarry I'd wandered into on my first night there.

When I thought of that I was on my feet, cursing myself for not finding the note sooner. It was a mile or more from Nantgarrew to the quarry and the only way for David to get there was to walk. And he'd walk, I was sure, the long way round, up the hill and along the ridge, not wanting to meet anybody on the way. There was just a slip of a chance that he hadn't got to the quarry yet. I rushed downstairs and out of the front door. There was nothing for it but to sprint down the valley road, hoping that my progress down the straight route would be faster than his over the hills. It wasn't until I'd started to run that I realised there might be a faster way.

Brigadier Moss's car was standing there, facing down the drive. The back seat was packed with files but this time

196

there was nobody standing guard. The young corporal had probably gone in for his supper. I glanced round. I'd driven a friend's car a few times, but that was several years ago and the experiment had not been a great success. I scrambled into the driving seat, trying to remember all you had to do to get the things started. Switch on petrol, that was easy enough. Check gear lever in neutral. Something called the advance and retard lever. I remembered vaguely that you had to set it in 'retard' to start, which seemed illogical enough to be right. Set hand throttle, hold breath, turn switch to on position. Nothing happened. I was getting out to start running again, cursing the wasted minute, until I remembered the other half of the process.

I went round to the front and opened the bonnet, fumbled my way through the procedure for flooding the carburetor. Then I closed the bonnet and grabbed the starting handle. No chance of quiet now, only speed. I cranked once, twice and the third time the engine spluttered into life and the whole car began to vibrate. As I threw myself back into the driving seat I heard shouts coming from the house, running feet on gravel. I glanced round and saw the corporal who usually drove the car rushing up, Jack Kelso not far behind.

'What are you doing? Stop. Stop her.'

I moved the advance and retard lever to 'advance', moved the other lever into what I devoutly hoped was first gear. Foot off clutch pedal and luckily onto accelerator and we were moving, though all too slowly. The driver's hand was on my shoulder, trying to pull me out of the seat. Then suddenly he wasn't there any more. I heard curses and shouts. Risking a glance back I saw two men wrestling on the gravel, then the running footsteps came after me again. The car was going no faster than a brisk walk and making a terrible noise although I had the accelerator pedal hard down. A figure drew level with me. I took one hand off the steering wheel and tried to push it away.

'Don't stop me. I'll explain later.'

He wouldn't be pushed, then I saw it wasn't the driver but Jack Kelso.

'Jack, I must have this thing.'

I thought he'd joined the opposition but then I heard, over the noise of the toiling engine, his reassuring Yorkshire voice.

'It might help if you got it out of first gear, Miss. Clutch down. That's it. Now the clutch again. If I get in there with you . . .'

I'd have accepted his company, but by then it was too late. The car leapt forward like a nervy horse and hurtled down the drive at a pace that even a horse would have found it hard to equal. I could still hear shouting behind me but it didn't matter any more. I negotiated the first bend, shot through the gap in the earthwork and over the cattle grid and saw the gateway at the end of the drive coming up at an indecent speed. The gate was open and I managed to get the car turned onto the road, although I think I caught one of the gateposts with the running board. It was a relief to see a clear road sloping down ahead of me. I operated the clutch again and yanked the gear lever up to its highest notch. The car responded by doubling its speed, or so it seemed to me. I had no goggles or hat so the rush of air sent my hair flapping free from its pins and brought tears to my eyes. It was some time before I could risk taking a hand off the wheel to wipe them, just in time to steer round a bend. When I saw what was in front of me, I let out a yell.

'Jenny, get out of the way!'

It seemed to be her fate, among other things, to be in the path of traffic on the valley road. She was just standing there, staring at me. I saw the reason for her panic. She recognised the car but couldn't expect me to be driving it. As far as she was concerned, it was Brigadier Moss himself coming after her. I pulled at the steering wheel and stamped on the brake, but neither seemed to operate quickly enough. We closed on Jenny, me yelling at her to get out of the way, she staring with open mouth. At the last minute two things happened. The car decided to obey orders and shift over to the right and Jenny came to her senses and jumped for the bank. I saw her lying there as I passed, a streak of blue dress and honey-coloured hair. She'd have to pick herself up. If I hadn't been helping Jenny to escape I might have seen David's note sooner. It wasn't a helpful thought and after the swerve I needed all my concentration to get the car sounding happy again and on a straight course. I could see Mrs Minter's house and the farm at Cymyoy in the distance. The turning to the old quarry must come before that. I couldn't afford to miss it.

I remembered the last time I'd been there a wooden gate had blocked the track from the valley road up to the quarry. I had only the haziest idea of how to stop and no time to go down through the sequence of gears. If necessary I'd simply turn the switch to 'off' and jump out as we came alongside the gate. With reasonable luck the car should stop rolling before it reached Abergavenny. I was getting ready for the jump when I saw that somebody had left the gate open. I wrenched the wheel and we turned in between the gateposts. There was an impact that slewed the car sideways, a sound of wrenching wood and metal, then we were going forwards again. I glanced down and saw that we'd left what remained of our right running board on the gatepost. But at least the impact and the fact that the track to the quarry went steeply uphill were slowing the vehicle to a manageable walking pace. I trod on the brake until it stopped, just a few yards before we ran into the back of Monica Minter's red car.

TWENTY-THREE

IT WAS DRAWN UP TIDILY at the side of the track, not abandoned like my wounded vehicle, but there was no sign of anybody near it. I couldn't imagine what Monica Minter might be doing there. For a moment I wondered if David might have stolen her car, as I'd stolen Brigadier Moss's, but decided he hadn't. Suicide, yes. Car theft, no. It looked like another complication at a time when I didn't need it. I walked past the car and up the track to the floor of the quarry.

There was nobody there. I was standing on small chippings of red stone with the quarry face rising in front of me, cut into deep steps like the seats in a Roman theatre. To my right was a small pool almost completely dried up by the heat, with clumps of sedge more brown than green. At the foot of the quarry was a mass of tumbled blocks of stone, casting deep shadows from the sun low down on the hills opposite. Some of the shadows looked so like a sprawled and lifeless man that I had to go up and touch them before I knew they weren't. I found myself stumbling from shadow to shadow, catching my feet in cracks, grazing palms, elbows and knuckles against the rocks. Nothing.

I stepped back and looked up at the top of the quarry, where a few clumps of grass overhung emptiness. Nobody visible, but if he'd been standing only a few yards back from the edge I couldn't see him. I wanted to call out, but if he were up there, making up his mind to jump, that might startle him into doing it. Besides, David was stubborn. It had always been hard to talk him out of anything. The best chance, if I could manage it, was to find him before he knew I was there. I looked at a quarryman's path that went zig-zagging up the face. Twenty feet or so above the quarry floor it crossed a stream that was no more than a streak of damp on a plank bridge, then went up from ledge to ledge. Steep but quite possible with a reasonable head for heights. As for Monica Minter, goodness knows where she was. I'd worry about that later.

I hitched my skirt into my belt and started up the path. As I got near the plank bridge I saw that somebody must have been across it not long before me. There was a damp patch the width of the plank and no more than six inches long showing that until recently the earth under it had been protected from the sun. On a day as hot as this the patch would have dried out within an hour or two. More than ever I wanted to call out to David, but stopped myself. Not trusting the bridge, since it had already moved once, I took the stream at a jump and went on up the path. It took a long swerve out to the right, then a hairpin bend round a boulder where I had to use my hands. Two-thirds of the way up now.

'Stop!'

The shout came from below. I looked down and there on the quarry floor, dead centre of the theatrical space, was Monica Minter in full regalia of red jacket, black skirt and black leather boots. She was also carrying her brother's revolver. Damn the woman. If anything could provoke David into jumping, she would. Any chance of keeping quiet was gone now. I shouted down to her:

'Go away. I'll talk to you later. Just go away now.'

'Come down, Nell Bray, and tell me what you have to tell me.'

Heaven help us, the woman had now gone completely mad.

'I don't know what you're talking about.'

I turned away, my attention on the path as it got steeper and narrower. Still no sight or sound of anybody up above.

'I said come down.'

201

A bullet thwacked against the quarry face a few yards in front of me. The explosion of the revolver went clattering round and round the quarry.

'Now will you come down?'

'No, damn you. There's a man's life in danger.'

'There's a man already dead, and you killed him.'

A second bullet struck, a few yards under my feet this time. Monica Minter, as might have been expected, seemed a reasonably efficient shot and against the quarry face I was a good target. There was nowhere to shelter and no point in ducking. I looked down at her.

'What do you mean, I killed him?'

At that point I thought she might have found David's body.

'I mean that you shot Colonel Ralph Keyson.'

The relief was so great that I laughed.

'You exult in it. You even laugh at it.'

She levelled the revolver again.

'Of course I didn't. Why in the world would I have wanted to shoot Ralph Keyson?'

'Because he knew about your activities, you and Dr Stroud and Dr Freud and the rest of your traitor friends.'

I was annoyed to be classed as a disciple of Dr Freud. I hoped to live long enough to have a chance to tell him one day what I thought of his theories which, in my recent experience, had caused nothing but trouble.

'This is no time to discuss psychology. I didn't kill him.'

'Then why did you send me this note?'

'For goodness sake, what note?'

With her free hand she took a piece of paper out of her pocket and waved it at me.

'I can't read it from up here. What's it supposed to say?'

'It says that if I met you here at the quarry you'd tell me who killed him.'

'I didn't write it.'

'You don't need to tell me. I worked it out for myself. It was you all the time.'

She was raving. I hoped it would affect her aim. I turned and went on walking up the path.

'If you won't come down, I'm coming up to you.'

I looked down. She was striding up the path towards the plank bridge, red scarf flapping, the gun steady in her hand. Then, as I looked down, I saw another streak of red and flash of metal, smaller and higher up, something that had nothing to do with Monica Minter's battle gear. The object was between her and me, propped between the plank bridge and the rock. It would be invisible from below but was quite clear from where I was standing. That wouldn't have mattered to the person who put it there because it had never been intended that it should be seen from above. As soon as anybody had set foot on the plank bridge the grenade would have been dislodged, the pressure taken off the lever. Three seconds after that it would have exploded in time to blow to fragments the person who'd just crossed the plank. It was the way they booby trapped trenches against the Germans, a soldier's trick.

When I saw it, Monica Minter was perhaps ten steps from the plank.

'Stop. Don't cross the bridge.'

She looked at me, levelled the gun. She'd taken it for a threat. Cursing her, I gathered myself and jumped from where I was standing to the zig-zag of path immediately below, losing ten feet or so of height in one bound. Small stones clattered.

'So you've decided to come down, have you?'

'Stay where you are. There's a grenade.'

She still thought I was threatening her. She came striding on to get at me. Neither running nor warning would help. I simply hurled myself down the slope at her, a one-woman avalanche in a welter of stone chippings. She shouted something, fired another shot but it must have gone wide. When I crashed into her, going rather faster than the best speed the car had managed, she was no more than three steps away from the plank.

My impact knocked her off her feet and we went rolling over and over together until I felt dampness on my back and gritty water in my mouth and realised we'd hit the muddy pond on the quarry floor. She'd landed beside me and, before she'd even got her breath back, began kicking at me. I tried to hold her down but realised I'd done some injury to my left shoulder. There was a gasp of pain from her as she tried to put her weight on her right elbow. The gun was nowhere in sight. It must have fallen among the rocks or been sunk in the mud. For a moment we just sat there beside each other, exhausted. Her face was red-grey from the mud and when she tried to say something her open mouth looked as startlingly pink as a kitten's. I suppose mine was the same.

'There was a grenade up there. If you'd stepped on that plank you'd have been blown to pieces.'

'Did you put it there?'

'No, of course not. It was the same person who killed Ralph Keyson, the one who'd already put a grenade in Dr Stroud's study.'

'Who?'

She didn't believe me even then. And, now it had come to it, I didn't want to tell her. I glanced up at the lip of the quarry and saw a head looking down at us. I couldn't make out the face, but I knew who it must be, the person who'd sent both of us notes to decoy us there. I pointed.

'Up there.'

She glanced up and the figure drew away from the edge. Whether I'd have gone chasing after it if I'd been on my own I still don't know. As it was, Monica Minter shouted and dragged herself upright, her uninjured arm pressing on my injured shoulder. I had to go after her or she'd have been straight up the quarry face and over the plank, in spite of what I'd said.

'Not that way, for goodness sake. There must be another path.'

But before we found it, the thing happened. A shape, like a bird of prey swooping, detached itself from the top of the quarry and hung dark against the peach-coloured sky. Then, as we watched, it turned itself from a bird into a human being and began to fall. It seemed to me that it fell slowly, like something in a dream, and I was rooted there, unable to do or feel anything. It came out of the light into the darkness of the quarry shadow and once the shadow caught it seemed to fall faster. Then there was a sound, a cry from Monica Minter and something lying sprawled across a slab of rock. After that cry there was silence. We both walked towards it but I got there first. He'd fallen on his back, neck bent at an impossible angle, but the face was unmarked. Either he'd taken his glasses off or lost them in the fall. She came up behind me.

'Dr Stroud.'

'Yes. Are you pleased? He was the enemy, wasn't he?'

She turned away and went behind a rock. I could hear her being sick. I decided to leave her to it and got myself along the quarry track, past the two vehicles to the road. I was sitting on the grass verge in the last of the daylight when Brigadier Moss's corporal, angry and footsore, came marching along the road at the double and found me.

TWENTY-FOUR

'AT THE VERY LEAST YOU stole War Office property. I believe it was a deliberate attempt to sabotage the war effort.'

Early next morning, after all that I'd told him, Brigadier Moss was still fretting over the temporary loss of his vehicle.

'If I really were trying to sabotage the war effort I'd make a better job of it than that. Your vehicle is still running perfectly well.'

It had, at any rate, brought me and the corporal back up the valley. This morning it had gone down again, with Dr Caspian and Jack Kelso as passengers, to retrieve Dr Stroud's body and deal with the unexploded grenade. Nobody had mentioned Jenny. I could only hope she was safely out of the way.

'In any case, I've saved you from a serious mistake. You were going to charge an innocent man with murder on the strength of a dream.'

'Dr Stroud has yet to be proved guilty.'

'Well get on and deal with it, or let the police do it. I've given you everything you need.'

'Why didn't you tell me you suspected it when you were talking to me this afternoon?'

'I wasn't certain then.' No need to tell him what the last piece of the jigsaw had been.

'And yet soon after that you stole my vehicle and went off to the quarry.'

'I hadn't expected to find Dr Stroud there. I was trying to stop David Ellward committing suicide. But as it turned out David was never anywhere near the quarry. Dr Stroud must have got him to write that note – goodness knows how – to decoy me there.'

'Why should he do that?'

'For exactly the same reason as he forged a note from me to Monica Minter to get her there. One of us, and I don't think he minded which, was to be killed by that grenade under the plank. The one who survived would get the blame for that and Ralph Keyson's murder as well.'

Brigadier Moss pressed his fingers hard against his forehead and closed his eyes.

'Why should he want to kill you or Mrs Minter?'

'I'm not sure that he really wanted to kill either of us, but somebody not connected with Nantgarrew had to take the blame. In her case, he knew she and Colonel Keyson had been spying on him, doing everything they could to discredit his work. As for me, I'd worked out how he could have planned that booby trap with the hand grenade in his study. Heaven help me, I even described to him how it was done.'

I remembered his eyes on me, listening as calmly to that as to anything else. Professional training.

'He admitted it?'

'He didn't have to. The problem was, at the time I was convinced that it was Ralph Keyson who'd set up the trap. After all, he'd done something very similar with Stanley Gorton in the conservatory. It was that trick that gave Dr Stroud his idea. Keyson really had only himself to blame. At the time of that so-called conservatory shooting, I think Dr Stroud was only considering murdering him. But Keyson had handed him something very close to an alibi.'

'In what sense?'

'Look, who were in that conservatory when the shot was apparently fired?'

'Lieutenant Gorton, Dr Stroud, Colonel Keyson.'

'Correct. So the assumption was that one of those three was the target. Again, who were the closest when that grenade went off in the study?'

'Dr Stroud and Colonel Keyson.'

'Exactly. So from his point of view it was worth building on Keyson's trick and going to some trouble to set up the grenade trap. He put the grenade in place, ran a wire from the wedge over the photo to the door handle and made sure that the door was left ajar when he went out to the hall to meet Keyson. Then all he had to do was pull the door towards him while they were standing there. Having, of course, taken care to write "Bollocks" on the *Orders for Patients* to distract Keyson's attention while he did it.'

Brigadier Moss made a note. I was sure that it was a reminder to have the notice de-bollocked as soon as our interview was over. When he'd finished the note he looked at me for a long time.

'If what you say is true, Miss Bray, then Dr Stroud was a very cold-blooded and evil man.'

'Certainly a cool-minded man, and a very ingenious one. Also, a brave man.'

'Brave!'

'Yes. He died defending something he believed in, even if he was mistaken. Tens of thousands of men are being forced to die for something they don't believe in.'

I could, I found, forgive Dr Stroud for trying to kill me with the grenade. As far as he was concerned, there was a war on. Nothing personal about it.

'And there's still no proof.'

'No?'

I'd retrieved the papers from the shed, the ones in Dr Stroud's handwriting. Now I put them on the desk in front of him.

'Read those.'

I watched him while he read. I'd taken them, when I first saw part of them, to be Dr Stroud's description of Stanley Gorton's state of mind when he was plotting murder. It had been much closer to home. It was a detailed description, up to the day he died, of his own killing of Keyson from the time the idea first came to him to the point where he trailed him along the ditch. After that the notes were less detailed, but he'd kept it up to date until a few hours before his death. He recorded his thoughts, his pulse-rate, his lack of libido. But there was a sadness running through it. Night after night his dream patrols went out but came back empty-handed. It seemed that through the planning of the murder and after it he didn't dream, or never remembered his dreams. He was, he decided, repressing them. Being guilty of repression, a sin against the Freudian creed, seemed to worry him far more than the fact of murder.

Brigadier Moss took a long time to read the notes. When he'd finished he asked just one question.

'How did you get these?'

'I found them on a bonfire.'

He let his hands flop down on the papers.

'Well. I think you may leave this with me, Miss Bray.'

'Not yet.'

'What do you mean, not yet?'

My shoulder was aching abominably and so was my head. It must have hit a rock or two on the way down the quarry.

'We have to discuss the future of Nantgarrew.'

'That's not something I'm prepared to discuss with you, but I think you may take it that Nantgarrew's future as a military hospital will not be a long one.'

'What will happen to the patients?'

'Those who still need treatment will be sent to appropriate establishments.'

'And the others?'

'Officers and men found fit to serve by a medical board will naturally rejoin their units.'

'At the front?'

'Yes, if that's where their units are serving.'

'I don't think that's a very good idea.'

It was the first time I'd actually heard anybody grinding his teeth.

'Oh you don't, don't you?'

'No. They were sent here in the first place because they were under severe mental strain. All the War Office has done to help them is put them under the charge of a murderer.'

That, I knew, was unfair to Dr Stroud who'd been a meticulous doctor by his lights. I told myself I was only doing what he'd have wanted.

'It was an experimental establishment.'

'Do you think that will make the public feel better about it?'

'We hardly intend to publicise this sad affair.'

'Perhaps I do. Perhaps I intend to let people know what the army sees fit to do with its sick men. Perhaps I intend to let them know that convalescent officers go to spy on other officers and hand out secret documents to old family friends.'

I could see his Adam's apple bulging and the neck muscles twitching inside his tight collar.

'I suppose you intend to publicise this interesting speculation in some pacifist magazine.'

'Yes, here – and in America.'

I could see from his face that I'd scored there. America had only just decided to come into the war and public opinion on the other side of the Atlantic was held to be delicate. I had friends there.

'Of course, if I knew the men from Nantgarrew weren't being sent back to the trenches, I might decide to delay publication for a while.'

I left him with that thought, and with Dr Stroud's records, and went outside. The gardening boy must have been waiting. He came running up to me, hot and dusty.

'Miss, there's a message, Miss.'

He handed me an envelope, grimed with his thumbprints. My name on the envelope was in Jenny's handwriting.

'Nell, I'm at Gwenda's. What's happening? Please come.'

I sighed. The boy was looking at me anxiously.

'Yesterday, did Dr Stroud give you a message to deliver to Mrs Minter?'

He nodded, looking scared.

'He's had an accident, Miss?'

'Yes.'

I read the note again. It was no good. I had to go to her. Another weary trudge.

'Mr Williams sent the pony, Miss.'

It was tied to a tree half way down the drive, a hairy little beast with a felt saddle and reins as stiff as dried seaweed. Still it plodded on through the heat and the clouds of flies down the valley road and didn't even flinch when Brigadier Moss's car toiled past on its way back to Nantgarrew. Jack and Dr Caspian were in front with the driver, a long shape wrapped in grey blankets on the back seat.

Jenny was sitting in the cool farm kitchen, with Gwenda and her mother, peeling vegetables. When she saw me she jumped up and led me into a side room. The window was open and the scent of hay came in, mingling with smells of cheese and bacon from the pantry.

'I know he's dead, Nell.'

'Yes. Do you know how?'

'They say he . . . fell. Down the quarry. Did he?'

'No. I'm afraid he jumped.'

'Thank you. I guessed, but thank you for telling me.'

Her face was quite calm but her hands were pressing against each other.

'How much else did you know?'

'I knew he must have killed Ralph Keyson. Right from the start. That night, I went to his room. He hadn't been talking to me for days, except about cases and then not much. I went to his room and he wasn't there. I went out to look for him. I didn't find him but I saw that Minter woman. It was after that I heard the shot, and I guessed.'

'You guessed immediately that Dr Stroud had shot Ralph Keyson. Why?'

'Because Keyson had found out about us. It was nothing much, Nell. It only lasted a week or two. But he spied on us, found out about it. It was cruel the way he treated Julius, kept dropping hints, threatening to tell Brigadier Moss but not doing it. Oh, he was an evil man, evil.'

'And yet you let me think it was Keyson who was your lover. I should have asked outright instead of trying to be tactful for once. An overrated virtue, tact.'

'But if you'd known about Julius and me, you'd have suspected.'

211

'Yes.'

'Nell, I hated deceiving you, but what could I do?'

'And yet it was you who brought me here in the first place.'

'I know, ironic wasn't it? I wonder who really fired that shot into the conservatory. Not that it matters now.'

I opened my mouth to tell her, then closed it again. If I did that we'd have to go into the whole business of Julius Stroud's meticulous planning for the murder. Better that Jenny should think of it as one desperate moment.

'On the road that night, when you bumped into Robin Duncan . . .?'

'I was running away Nell, just running away. When I saw somebody coming after me on a bicycle I thought it was Julius, running away too.'

No wonder she'd been almost out of her mind with panic that night. Dr Stroud had been much the cooler of the two, remembering to bring the murder weapon with him in his coat pocket when he went with me to find the body.

'Would it have mattered so much, Jenny, if he really had told the authorities about you?'

'The officer commanding a military hospital, having sexual relations with one of his staff? It would have closed Nantgarrew. Look at the fuss he made about poor Gwenda.'

She glanced towards the room next door.

'And now it will close anyway.'

'I suppose it will. It's a terrible setback for Freudian psychoanalysis in Britain.'

I said nothing to that.

'Does Brigadier Moss know about me?'

'About your being here? No. But I think you should go to London as I told you.'

If he or the police really decided to pick over the remains, she might still be regarded as an accomplice. I thought Brigadier Moss would decide in the end to let them lie, but Jenny would be best out of the way.

'All right, Nell. I'll go this afternoon. I wanted to see somebody in London anyway.'

I was suspicious of this docility.

'Who?'

'A woman I know who's organising women's ambulance teams for the front. She needs drivers and . . .'

'Jenny, are you quite out of your mind?'

The wave of my arm sent bunches of drying herbs swinging. The murmur of conversation from Gwenda and her mother next door stopped and started again, self-consciously. I lowered my voice.

'If you have some idiotic idea of going out to get killed to make amends, forget it. You're not safe on foot, let alone driving an ambulance.'

Some colour came to her face.

'It's not that. I've nothing to make amends for. I think it's simply time to objectivise some of my internal conflicts.'

I understood at that moment how Brigadier Moss must feel faced with me.

'For goodness sake, isn't that what the whole of Europe's doing already? All right, go if you must, but for heaven's sake be careful. We need some people with intelligence left after this war.'

She came out to see me off. I'd begged the loan of the pony again to get back up the valley. The gardening boy could ride it down again next day. When I got back to Nantgarrew at last Jack Kelso was there by the bottom of the drive. He held the bridle while I dismounted.

'I'll see to him, Miss. You look all in.'

He seemed remarkably cheerful. Perhaps it was the effect of being reunited with one of his grenades. We walked up the drive together, Jack leading the pony.

'So we're all off on our travels, Miss.'

'I suppose so.'

'Can't say I'll be sorry. In fact, I took the liberty of having a word with the Brigadier. He's not such a bad sort after all.'

'Brigadier Moss?'

Still, if he'd already found a safe billet for Jack I was prepared to forgive him a lot.

'Yes. He thinks he can do something. There's the medical board to square and so on, but that shouldn't be too difficult.'

'Good.'

'So if all goes well I could be back with my own lot in France in a couple of weeks.'

I stared at him over the pony's back.

'The whole world's mad.'

'Yes, Miss, so you might as well be with your friends.'

After a few more steps I said: 'That gun you all took such trouble with, did you know it was Dr Stroud who put it there?'

'Not at the time. I did wonder about it later.'

'So you guessed Dr Stroud shot him?'

'Well, in the end I worked out he was one of the two front runners.'

'Who was the other one?'

He grinned.

'It did cross my mind that it might have been you, Miss. No offence of course.'

There seemed nothing more to say. Further up the drive he gave me his usual half-wave, half-salute and plodded off with the pony towards the pasture.

I found David just where he'd been when I last saw him, sitting alone in the common room playing the hurdy-gurdy tune on the piano. He said, without turning his head:

'So it was Dr Stroud?'

'Yes.'

I took from my pocket his note about climbing up and not climbing down again and put it on the music rest in front of him. He didn't miss a note.

'Where did you find that? It's from my dream record.'

'Dream record?'

'Yes. I got into the habit of writing down my dreams as soon as I woke up so that I didn't miss any details.'

'And you gave your notes to Dr Stroud?'

'Of course. I'll miss discussing my dreams with him.'

'He used your dreams. He tried to use them to gain time for himself. Don't you feel angry with him?'

He played another phrase.

'Angry? What's the point? As for using our dreams – doesn't everybody do that?'

I stood up.

'I'm sorry Nell. I've annoyed you. Anyway, I've got some good news for you – if you think it's good.'

'What?'

'The Brigadier tells me he doesn't think I'll be needed back in France, not for some time at least. Apparently there's an instructor's job somewhere in England that calls for my invaluable qualities.'

He gave me a twisted smile over his shoulder.

'I haven't thanked you, have I Nell? Thank you for being so anxious to save my life, such as it is.'

'Oh, don't mention it.'

'I wish I could do something for you. I'd like to. Perhaps I should say what the village girls say to the soldiers in France: "*Peut-être – après la guerre*".'

Under his fingers the hurdy-gurdy, for a bar or two, took on a more hopeful sound.

'Perhaps, then, after the war.'

I left before he could get it back to a minor key.